Loose Ends

A PLAY

By Michael Weller

Samuel French, Inc.

also by
MICHAEL WELLER . . .

THE BALLAD OF SOAPY SMITH

FISHING

MOONCHILDREN

NOW THERE'S JUST THE THREE OF US

SPLIT

Consult our *Basic Catalogue of Plays* for details.

Loose Ends

A PLAY

By Michael Weller

SAMUEL FRENCH, INC.
45 WEST 25TH STREET   NEW YORK 10010
7623 SUNSET BOULEVARD   HOLLYWOOD 90046
LONDON   *TORONTO*

CIRCLE IN THE SQUARE

THEODORE MANN
Artistic Director

PAUL LIBIN
Managing Director

presents

KEVIN KLINE
ROXANNE HART

in

LOOSE ENDS

a new play by

MICHAEL WELLER

with

ERNEST ABUBA	**JEFF BROOKS**	**MICHAEL KELL**	**MICHAEL LIPTON**
PATRICIA RICHARDSON	**JAY O. SANDERS**	**STEVE VINOVICH**	**CEL WEST**

Scenery by
ZACK BROWN

Costumes by
KRISTINA WATSON

Lighting by
DAVID F. SEGAL

Photographs by
CECILIA VETTRAINO

Hairstyles by
MICHAEL WASULA

Directed by

ALAN SCHNEIDER

Originally Produced by
Arena Stage, Washington, D.C.

The Circle in the Square productions are partially assisted by public funds from the New York Sta on the Arts, the City of New York and the National Endowment for the Arts. The productions are also by grants from the Ford Foundation and The Andrew W. Mellon Foundation.
The Producers and the Theatre Management of the Circle in the Square
are members of the League of New York Theatres and Producers, Inc.

CAST
(in order of appearance)

PAUL	Kevin Kline
SUSAN	Roxanne Hart
JANICE	Patricia Richardson
BALINESE FISHERMAN	Ernest Abuba
DOUG	Jay O. Sanders
MARAYA	Celia Weston
BEN	Steve Vinovich
SELINA	Jodi Long
RUSSELL	Michael Kell
LAWRENCE	Michael Lipton
PHIL	Jeff Brooks

Scene 1
A beach in Bali. 1970.

Scene 2
Doug and Maraya's yard in New Hampshire. 1971.

Scene 3
Back yard of Paul and Susan's apartment house in Boston.
1973.

Scene 4
Paul and Susan's living room, Boston. 1974.

Scene 5
Central Park, New York. 1975.

Scene 6
Paul and Susan's living room on Central Park West. 1977.

Scene 7
The terrace of Paul and Susan's apartment, Central Park
West. 1978.

Scene 8
A cabin in New Hampshire. 1979.

5

PRODUCTION NOTE

In its original production the scene changes of LOOSE ENDS were accompanied by photographs. These showed scenes from Paul and/or Susan's life in the spans of time between the dates of each scene. Two things were accomplished by this. The audience's attention was taken off the stage where, in-the-round, there was nothing to hide from view the frantic scurrying of cast and crew while pieces of scenery were changed. And, more important, the pictures supplied information about the world of Paul and Susan and their friends. They were not intended to represent photographs taken by Susan. Their point of view, so to speak, was neutral.

Each scene ended with the actors freezing in position on stage as the lights dimmed and a slide of those actors in that position was projected on a screen. The photograph had been taken in a 'real life' equivalent of the stage set. During the scene change there followed numbers of slides taken in various settings never seen in the play, then as a scene change was ending, we concluded with a slide of the next scene with actors in position. When stage lights came up we saw the theatrical equivalent of the last slide. There were no slides at the beginning and end of each act.

CHARACTER DESCRIPTIONS

PAUL BAUMER—25-30 male lead, sensitive, earnest.

SUSAN STEEN—25-30 female lead, bright, attractive, sensitive.

JANICE—25-30, Susan's friend, a crazy, nice girl.

BALINESE FISHERMAN—Young native.

DOUG—25-30, country type, wry humor.

MARAYA—25-30, Doug's woman, also country, earthy, off-beat humor.

BEN BAUMER—36, Paul's older brother, slick, successful Madison Avenue type. (35-40 yrs.)

SELINA—Chinese-American, 25-30.

RUSSELL—mid to late 20's, Janice's guru boyfriend, a bit odd, has a sort of brooding quality about him.

LAWRENCE—30ish, an art director, homosexual, garrulous and charming.

PHIL—Janice's husband, square but not unsympathetic.

CAST

PAUL

SUSAN

JANICE

BALINESE FISHERMAN

DOUG

MARAYA

BEN

SELINA

RUSSELL

LAWRENCE

PHIL

8

Loose Ends

Scene 1

*Slide: 1970. A beach. Night. Full Moon. Waves. On
bare stage,* PAUL *and* SUSAN, *early mid-20's, naked,
clothes around. He sits facing ocean (us) and she
lies curled up.*

PAUL. It was great at the beginning. I could speak the
language almost fluently after a month and the people
were fantastic. They'd come out and help us. Teach us
songs. Man, we thought it was all going so well. But
we got all the outhouses dug in six months and we had
to stay there two years, that was the deal. And that's
when we began to realize that none of the Nglele were
using these outhouses. We'd ask them why and they'd
just shrug. So we started watching them very carefully
and what we found out was the Nglele use their feces
for fertilizer. It's like gold to them. They thought we
were all fucking crazy expecting them to waste their
precious turds in our spiffy new outhouses. Turns out
they'd been helping us because they misunderstood why
we were there. They thought it was some kind of
punishment and we'd be allowed to go home after we
finished digging the latrines, that's why they were helping us and then when we stayed on they figured we
must be permanent outcasts or something and they just
stopped talking to us altogether. Anyway, me and Jeff,
the guy I told you about, we figured maybe we could
salvage something from the fuckup so we got a doctor
to make a list of all the medicines we'd need to start a

9

kind of skeleton health program in Ngleleland and we
ordered the medicine, pooled both our salaries for the
two years to pay for it. Paid for it. Waited. Never
came. So we went to the capitol to trace it and found
out this very funny thing. The Minister of Health and
confiscated it at the dock, same man who got our team
assigned to the Nglele Tribal Territories in the first
place. We were furious, man, we stormed into his office
and started yelling at him. Turned out to be a real nice
guy. Educated in England, British accent and everything. Had this office lined with sets of Dickens and
Thackeray all in leather bindings. Unbelievable. Anyway, he said he couldn't help us about the medicine
he'd been acting on orders from higher up, which we
knew was bullshit, then he said he really admired our
enthusiasm and our desire to help his people but he
wanted to know just out of curiosity, if we'd managed
to start the medical program and save a thousand lives,
let's say, he wanted to know if we were prepared to
feed and clothe those thousand people for the next ten
years, twenty years, however long they lived. He made
us feel so god damned naive, so totally helpless and un-
prepared, powerless. We went out of there, got drunk,
paid the first women we could find and spent the rest
of the week fucking our brains out. And then for the
next year and two months we just sat around in
Ngleleland stoned out of our minds counting off the
days we had left before we could go home. Anyway,
since you asked, that's what the Peace Corps was like.

SUSAN. Sounds pretty shitty.

PAUL. Well. At least now I speak fluent Nglele. You
never know when that'll come in handy in Philadelphia.

SUSAN. You got another cigarette? (PAUL *finds his
shirt, get out cigarettes, lights two of them.*) I got this
American newspaper yesterday, they sell 'em at that

hotel by the market place, they're about a week old
but I just wanted to read a newspaper . . . It was so
weird. I took it back to the shack . . . Oh, we rented
this shack just down the beach . . . me and Janice,
she's the girl you saw me with . . . (PAUL *hands cigarette to* SUSAN.) thanks . . . I should stop . . . anyway, I made a cup of coffee and sat on the beach and
read this paper. And, you know, all the stories were out
of date and I didn't know what most of 'em were about
anyway because we've been travelling for over a
month and I just started thinking, you know, all this
news could be from another planet, you know what I
mean, like is this stuff they're writing about happening
on the planet earth because I live on earth, I'm sitting
right here, right on the earth and none of this stuff is
happening to me. I just thought of that while you were
talking. I don't know why. Do you ever think about
things like that? (PAUL *starts chuckling.*) What? What
are you laughing at?

PAUL. Nothing.

SUSAN. You do that a lot, you know.

PAUL. Do what?

SUSAN. You start laughing when something isn't
funny and when I ask you what you're laughing at you
say "nothing."

PAUL. It's just. I don't know. I was just thinking I
spent two years going through a lot of very weird stuff
but when I try to talk about it it's just a story, just
some stuff that happened and now it's over. It doesn't
mean anything anymore.

SUSAN. That's not funny.

PAUL. No. No, it isn't.

SUSAN. You want me to tell you about something
weird that happened to me? You know, that way we'll
each have weird stories about each other.

PAUL. Sure. Go ahead.

SUSAN. O.K. When I was ten. No, eleven, I had my tonsils out and my dad was on a business trip, but I really wanted him to see my tonsils, so I made the doctor promise to put them in formaldehyde and I took them home. But they were real ugly and I decided I didn't want him to see them after all so I made a little fire in the back yard and said a few prayers and had a tonsil cremation and then I put the ashes in this vase on the mantelpiece. That was my big secret. It was really great because wherever I went I knew something that no one else knew and that seemed like something very important. I don't know why exactly. Then the maid cleaned the vase one day and that was that. Except that a year later the maid choked to death and they found two grapes lodged in her trachea, so I knew my tonsils had their revenge. I'm kidding. How long are you staying here?

PAUL. In Bali?

SUSAN. Yeah.

PAUL. I have a job that starts in two weeks.

SUSAN. Where?

PAUL. Philadelphia.

SUSAN. What kind of a job?

PAUL. Teaching English at this private school.

SUSAN. Is that what you're going to do? Teach English? I mean, you know, sort of forever?

PAUL. It's all I could get for now.

SUSAN. Do you know what you're going to do?

PAUL. When I grow up, you mean?

SUSAN. Yeah, you know.

PAUL. We'll see. What about you?

SUSAN. Oh, I don't know. I guess I'll travel with Janice for a while. Then I'll probably go home and do something or other that'll make me incredibly rich and respected and happy and fulfilled in every possible way and then, let's see, I'll move to the country and buy a little house with lots of stained glass and two cats, oh, and a solar heating panel and . . . . and a servant called Lothar or something like that . . . I don't know.

PAUL. Sounds nice.

SUSAN. Want to go in again?

PAUL. Do you?

SUSAN. I asked first.

PAUL. Sure.

SUSAN. O.K. (*They stand, remove clothes.*)

PAUL. Ready? One . . . two . . . three . . . GO! (PAUL *runs forward.* SUSAN *doesn't.* PAUL *stops, turns.* SUSAN *laughs.* PAUL *chases her down the beach, Off-stage. Shrieks, happy yelling.* SUSAN *runs back on.* PAUL *catches her. Tickle, kiss, passion. They roll on sand, kissing. Stop. Roll apart. They are full.*) This is incredible. Fucking incredible.

SUSAN. Listen, what do you think if . . . me and Janice made a pact that if anything happened while we were on this trip it was O.K. to split up and go on alone. And I like her, you know, she's a good friend, but she's into this whole thing about a guru she heard about in India, that's kind of how this trip started in the first place, but I like it right here and I was thinking maybe . . . I mean, if I told her to go on alone would you like to stay here for a while, see how things worked out and if it feels good maybe we could travel together, you know. Does that sound good? Paul?

PAUL. I have this job.

SUSAN. You didn't sound too enthusiastic about it.

PAUL. I'm not. That's not the point. I'm broke.

SUSAN. It doesn't cost anything to travel, you know. You can live for nothing if you do it right.

PAUL. Yeah, I guess so.

SUSAN. And I got a little saved up.

PAUL. I couldn't do that . . .

SUSAN. Why not? I mean, well, O.K. It's up to you.

PAUL. Is it? Yeah, I guess it is. I could just do it, couldn't I. I could just say fuck it. And I'd love to, jesus god would I ever love to. (*Pause.*) I don't believe this is happening. I really don't. (*They giggle.* PAUL *suddenly alert.*)

SUSAN. What's that?

PAUL. I heard something. (*They peer into darkness.*) Over there, look, someone's coming. There's a flashlight. (*They start dressing quickly.*) Hello! Hello! Who's there? (*Flashlight beam on them.*) Americans. We're Americans. Tourists. Who is it?

JANICE. (*Offstage.*) Susan, is that you?

SUSAN. Shit.

PAUL. What's the matter?

SUSAN. It's Janice. My friend.

JANICE. Are you all right? (*Enter* JANICE *with flashlight.*)

SUSAN. What are you doing?

JANICE. I just wondered what happened to you.

SUSAN. I went for a walk.

JANICE. I just got worried, that's all. You said you'd be back by five.

SUSAN. Things happened.

JANICE. Yeah, 'cause it's almost ten. I got worried.

SUSAN. This is Paul.

PAUL. Hi.

JANICE. Hi. So, are you coming back?

SUSAN. Janice, what's the matter with you?

JANICE. Someone was walking around outside the shack. I heard footsteps. I didn't want to stay back there. I mean a tourist did get killed here, you know.

PAUL. Wasn't that last year?

JANICE. The point is, it *can* happen.

PAUL. I thought I heard his wife killed him.

JANICE. Susan, I don't want to go back there alone. Those blue spiders are all over the place tonight. I tried to spray with a bug bomb, but it just makes the legs come off and they keep moving around. Please, Susan, I know it's a drag, I know we decided to be loose about the travelling, but I don't want to go back to that place by myself.

SUSAN. Can we talk about this later?

JANICE. Yes, I think we should do that, Susan.

SUSAN. Good night, Janice. (JANICE *turns to go. Screams. Drops flashlight.*)

JANICE. Oh my God. (*They look. Nearby stands a Balinese holding a large fish.*)

SUSAN. Who's that? (BALINESE *advances with a smile, holds the fish out.*)

BALINESE. (*Something in Balinese.*)

JANICE. Oh, Jesus, it's him again.

SUSAN. Who?

JANICE. He's been following me around all day. He was in the market place. What do you want?

BALINESE. (*Something in Balinese.*)

JANICE. I don't understand you. I don't speak your language. Please go away.

PAUL. Is that fish for us?

BALINESE. (*Something in Balinese.*)

PAUL. Are you trying to sell the fish? You want money? Dollars. Dollars? (PAUL *goes towards* BALI-NESE *reaching into pocket for money.* BALINESE *backs away and holds fish from him.*)

BALINESE. (*Something in Balinese.*)

PAUL. O.K., O.K., take it easy. (BALINESE *kneels before* JANICE *and proffers fish.*)

BALINESE. (*Something in Balinese.*)

JANICE. (*Pause.*) Let's just buy the fish, O.K.?

SUSAN. What are we gonna do with a fish. We don't even have a place to cook it.

JANICE. We'll make a fire on the beach, I don't care. Let's just get rid of him.

PAUL. I think I read somewhere that the Balinese offer a fish when they're in love. Seriously, I think he's proposing marriage.

JANICE. O.K., mister, look, I've had enough of this. Get up, I'll buy your fish, O.K. Buy. Money. Then you go away and leave me alone. Do you understand me. Comprenez? Shit.

BALINESE. (*Something in Balinese.*)

JANICE. You go away. Away. You go away.

BALINESE. Ooo gow weh.

JANICE. Here. (JANICE *hands money to* BALINESE *and takes fish.*) . . . Now you go. Go. (BALINESE *backs away then stands watching.*) No. Go all the way. Go completely away. All the way. (BALINESE *backs away into the night.*)

PAUL. He's gone.

JANICE. No he's not. He's just waiting out there. As soon as we start back he'll follow us.

SUSAN. Janice, I wish you'd cool it.

JANICE. I'm telling you, he's been after me all day.

SUSAN. All right, all right. He's gone now.

JANICE. Are you coming back?

SUSAN. Yes, I'm coming back. In a few minutes.

JANICE. It's really great to find out who your friends are. (*Exits.*)

PAUL. Good night . . .

SUSAN. Oh, man she is crazy. I mean I knew she could get a little weird sometimes, but this is ridiculous. This is a mistake. This trip is definitely a mistake.

PAUL. She seems O.K.

SUSAN. You don't have to travel with her. Do you have another cigarette? (PAUL *lights one for her.*) I was feeling so good. Was that really true about the fish?

PAUL. No.

SUSAN. (*Laughs.*) I like you.

PAUL. You have a pen?

SUSAN. What for?

PAUL. Get your address. Maybe I'll see you back in the States.

SUSAN. But I thought . . . ?

PAUL. I can't. I mean, yeah sure, I could. I could. But I can't. It's ridiculous. I mean, look at what I have after two years. A bunch of stories and a ticket home. I have to do something now. You know, where I end up with something I can . . . something that doesn't just go away, you know what I mean?

SUSAN. Hey, that's O.K. You don't have to explain it. I had a good time.

PAUL. Yeah.

SUSAN. You want to come back to the shack? I got a pen there. You can stay tonight if you want, there's room.

PAUL. I have to confirm a flight back at the hotel.

SUSAN. You're staying at the hotel?

PAUL. After two years in Ngleleland, are you kidding?

SUSAN. Does it have a shower? I got sand everywhere.

PAUL. Want to come back?

SUSAN. If it's O.K.

PAUL. Sure. (*They start out.* SUSAN *stops.*)

SUSAN. Shit.

PAUL. What's the matter?

SUSAN. I can't leave her alone. Janice, jesus. Look, I'll tell you what. Why don't I meet you at the hotel tomorrow. We could rent a couple of bikes and go out to the mountains . . .

PAUL. I'm leaving in the morning.

SUSAN. Oh. You didn't say. O.K. Well, I'm in the Denver phone book. Steen. That's two ees. We're the only Steens. That's my family.

PAUL. O.K., Susan Steen. Two ees.
SUSAN. What's your last name?
PAUL. Baumer.
SUSAN. Paul Baumer.
PAUL. Right.
SUSAN. So. Maybe I'll see you.
PAUL. O.K. Take it easy. (PAUL *and* SUSAN *stand for a moment. They exit in opposite directions. Fade.*)

SCENE 2

Slide: 1971. DOUG *and* MARAYA's *yard. Noon. On one side of stage rear end of a shingle covered trailer home on cinderblocks. Some shingles have fallen off and you can see painted metal beneath. There is a window in rear end. At other side of stage is nearly completed 2x4 frame for part of house. Tools, etc.* DOUG *and* PAUL, *stripped to waist, working on frame.*

DOUG. Listen, man, I've been there, you don't have to tell me about horny. Shit, when I found out ole Maraya was pregnant with baby-Jake I got a hard on—wouldn't go down for six months. Everything got me off and I mean everything. Even ole Doofus the dog. Even looking at flowers.
PAUL. Well, what I was . . .
DOUG. Man, there was this one time it was raining and I was walking home from the swimming hole and I just started thinking wow, this rain reminds me of Maraya's big ole tummy. Don't ask me why. And before I knew what I was doing there I was standing in the rain, standing, man, holding my pecker in my hand, pumping away just like I was in the shower or something, I don't know. This dude came driving right

by, I didn't give a shit, nothing was gonna stop me. He gets about fifty yards down the road and hits the brakes, tires screeching all over the place when he realizes he's just seen a sex maniac whacking off in the rain. I'm telling you, man, when the feeling hits you like that, fuck holding back, right.

PAUL. Yeah, but the thing is . . .

DOUG. I don't know. Maybe I'm just getting weird living up here. I'm not saying I'd ever go back to the city, ungh-uh, you can have that shit, but still . . . (PAUL *hands him piece of 2x4.*) What's this one for? Oh, yeah, Damn, I interrupted you again. I *am* getting weird, I'm telling you. Cisco came up here a couple weeks ago, stayed for two days, I couldn't stop talking. Nobody up here talks. How do I seem?

PAUL. What do you mean?

DOUG. Since the last time you saw me. Do I seem any weirder?

PAUL. No.

DOUG. You do.

PAUL. What do you mean?

DOUG. I don't know. So you're walking on this beach in Bali and you see this chick, right?

PAUL. Well, you know, we started talking and it felt really good. I mean after two years in Africa it felt really good to be talking to someone again . . .

DOUG. So you whipped out the big boy and shagged her on the beach.

PAUL. Douglas, you have a mind like a sewer, you know that.

DOUG. You didn't fuck her? You mean I been listening to all this shit for nothing?

PAUL. You haven't been listening, you've been talking the whole time.

DOUG. O.K., you got five minutes to get to the fuck or I'm quitting for lunch.

PAUL. You want to hear this or not?

DOUG. Shit, man, she really got to you, huh?

PAUL. I guess you could say that.

DOUG. And I did. So it's real serious, huh?

PAUL. Well, you know, for now. What do you want me to say?

DOUG. You don't know if it's serious?

PAUL. We'll see.

DOUG. O.K., you go to bed at night sometimes and you lie there together but you don't feel like you *have* to fuck before you go to sleep, right.

PAUL. What are you talking about?

DOUG. Just answer me, does that ever happen?

PAUL. Sure, sometimes.

DOUG. Then it's serious. So you fucked her on the beach. Hey, O.K., I'm sorry, what happened?

PAUL. I've been trying to tell you.

DOUG. Well I been waiting for it to get interesting. I can't help it if you don't know how to tell a story.

PAUL. O.K., look, the school closed . . .

DOUG. What school . . .

PAUL. Doug!

DOUG. What school? You didn't say anything about a school.

PAUL. Philadelphia. Where you wrote me that time?

DOUG. Oh, yeah. How come it closed?

PAUL. Oh, you know, it was one of those experimental places, develop the inner person, that kind of shit. Anyway, the parents must've got wise or something 'cause the school ran out of money halfway through the year and they had to close down. So there's me out of a job, nothing to do, so I got a bus up to Boston to check out a few possibilities and she was on the bus.

DOUG. You're shitting?

PAUL. I swear. I couldn't believe it.

Doug. You didn't even know she was back in America? That's really far out. I mean that's definitely in the land of spooky events.

Paul. Well, actually, I left out the part where I called her family in Denver and found out she was living in Boston.

Doug. Why you little devil.

Paul. I mean I wasn't sure I was going to try to look her up or anything. In fact I had a little thing going in Philadelphia and I wasn't even sure I wanted to leave.

Doug. Listen.

Paul. What?

Doug. She's real cute. I like her. Really. And I want to get back to the part where you fucked on the beach. And I want a sandwich. You want a sandwich?

Paul. You're never gonna get this house built.

Doug. Fuck the house, man, I'm hungry. (*Calls.*) MARAYA! (Maraya *appears in rear window of trailer.*)

Maraya. What do you want?

Doug. What's for food? We're getting hungry.

Maraya. It's not ready yet.

Doug. How 'bout a couple of beers?

Maraya. Get 'em yourself, I'm not your waitress.

Doug. I won't build your house. (Maraya *withdraws her head.*) Want a beer?

Paul. Sure.

(Doug *goes towards the trailer, passes* Susan *who is coming out. She has a camera over shoulder. She is eating an apple.*)

Doug. Beer my dear?

Susan. Lunch is coming in a minute.

Doug. There goes that darn Doug, ruining his appetite again. (Doug *goes into trailer.* Susan *comes to* Paul.)

SUSAN. How's it going?

PAUL. Pretty slow.

SUSAN. Maraya told me about this waterfall where you can go swimming. It's only about a mile. You want to go after lunch?

PAUL. Come here.

SUSAN. What?

PAUL. I want to go right now.

SUSAN. You want to go after lunch.

PAUL. Sure.

SUSAN. It's nice here.

PAUL. Do you like them?

SUSAN. Yeah. Maraya's a little weird with that baby, but I like them.

PAUL. Are you O.K.?

SUSAN. Sure.

PAUL. You seem a little, I don't know . . . something or other.

SUSAN. I always am a little something or other.

PAUL. Am I supposed to leave it alone? Am I supposed to not push it?

SUSAN. Babe, I'm fine, really.

PAUL. O.K. It's just, sometimes I'm not sure how you're feeling, that's all.

SUSAN. Don't worry about it.

PAUL. In other words, something's on your mind but you don't feel like talking about it right now?

SUSAN. It's nothing, really. I'm fine. Let's change the subject.

PAUL. O.K.

SUSAN. We'll talk about it later.

PAUL. O.K.

(DOUG *comes from trailer with three beers.*)

DOUG. Maraya wants to know, lunch out here or in the west wing?

PAUL. Out here's fine.

DOUG. Did I interrupt something?

PAUL. No, no.

DOUG. (*Yells.*) OUT HERE, AND HURRY UP, I GOTTA GO GET THAT BATTERY FOR THE TRUCK.

MARAYA. (*Offstage. Yells.*) IT'LL BE THERE WHEN IT'S READY.

DOUG. I'm gonna haveta start whuppin' that woman if she don't behave herself better. (DOUG *sits by* PAUL.) How come you didn't finish the house? (*Apple in mouth,* SUSAN *backs away and take pictures of* PAUL *and* DOUG *together.* DOUG *clowns.*)

SUSAN. Hey, come on, just relax, I want to get you two together. Just act natural.

DOUG. (*In a weird pose.*) I'm stuck, I can't move.

SUSAN. Doug. (DOUG *relaxes.*) O.K., now move a little closer.

DOUG. (*Moves closer.*) Don't get fresh.

(*Enter* MARAYA *from trailer carrying* BABY-JAKE *in one arm and balancing a plate of sandwiches with her free hand. She sees what's going on and stops, talks to* BABY-JAKE.)

MARAYA. Look, honey, they're taking pictures, see? That little thing she's holding goes click and that makes a picture and then you have something to look at so you can remember how it used to be. Done?

SUSAN. Yeah. (SUSAN *shoulders camera.* MARAYA *sets plate down.*)

MARAYA. O.K., troops, dig in.

BABY-JAKE. (*Cries.*)

(MARAYA *takes out breast and feeds* BABY-JAKE.)

SUSAN. How much did you pay for this place?

DOUG. Fifteen. It's eleven acres. Goes right down to the bluestone quarry in back and then over to the woods that way. Be worth about sixty/seventy when the house is finished and you figure inflation. You guys looking for something.

SUSAN. I was just wondering. It's nice up here.

DOUG. Listen, there's a place coming on the market soon, no one knows about it yet, state land on three sides so no one can build. I'll check it out for you if you're interested. It'd be great if you guys moved up here. Want me to check it out?

MARAYA. (*To* BABY-JAKE.) Ouch, honey, you're biting really hard, you know. You shouldn't do that 'cause it just makes my nipples sore and I get all tense and that stops the milk from flowing and you'll just get angrier. It's a vicious circle.

DOUG. You want me to check out that land?

PAUL. (*To* SUSAN.) What do you think?

SUSAN. I don't know. You want to?

PAUL. Do you?

SUSAN. I asked first.

PAUL. (*To* DOUG.) Sure. Why not?

DOUG. Hot damn, all right, you got it. This afternoon. Shit, I gotta get that battery. (*Stands.*) Who's coming to town? (*No one moves.*) Gee, I don't know if I'll have room for all of you.

PAUL. We're going to the waterfall.

DOUG. The waterfall, eh. We all know what happens at the waterfall, ho-ho. How 'bout you, Marsie, want to come to town?

MARAYA. I gotta do some stuff. Can you get me some smokes? Two packs. I'm trying to cut down, that's for all week. They say you can taste it in the milk, but I think that's bullshit. You can't taste it, can you honey? No, of course not.

Doug. (*To* Paul.) Give me a push down the hill, wouldya. (Paul *and* Doug *exit*.)

Susan. Do you mind if I take a few pictures?

Maraya. No, that'd be great.

Susan. Just stay like that. Don't worry about anything. (Susan *takes pictures*.)

Maraya. Hey, I really like that thing you gave us with the guy dancing.

Susan. Oh, right. I got 'em in Tibet. It's a woodcut on silk.

Maraya. Did you buy a lot of 'em? I bet you could sell 'em.

Susan. That's what I did. Sold about a hundred of them. They only cost like a dollar each in Tibet.

Maraya. How much you get for 'em, if you don't mind my asking?

Susan. Twenty-five.

Maraya. Far out.

Susan. Yeah, that's how I got all this camera stuff. I went on a real splurge. Hold that, yeah, like that, that's nice.

Maraya. Oww, shit Jake, you're getting obnoxious, come on. Hold still. She's taking our picture.

Susan. Why don't you try the other one?

Maraya. What other one? Oh. (Maraya *gives* Baby-Jake *the other teat*.) Is that kind of a serious trip, the photography?

Susan. Oh, I don't know. I enjoy it.

Maraya. You're taking a lot of pictures, is why I asked. Hey, this is a lot better, you know. He's not biting. I can't wait'll he can talk. It's weird 'cause you know he's got a lotta stuff on his mind, you can tell he's thinking about things all the time, but you can't ask him about it. It's really frustrating. Are you gonna have kids?

Susan. Probably. Someday. I don't know.

MARAYA. You should have 'em pretty soon though. They come out healthier when you have 'em young and if you wait too long you might get a mutation. You'd probably be a good mother.

SUSAN. Why do you say that?

MARAYA. I don't know, just a feeling. Like how you knew about changing the breast. (*Pause.*) You guys living together?

SUSAN. We're getting a place back in Boston this fall. Supposedly.

MARAYA. You sound sort of like you're not too sure.

SUSAN. Oh, you know. If we do, we do, if we don't we don't.

MARAYA. I know what you mean. (SUSAN *is looking at* MARAYA.) What are you looking at?

SUSAN. Did you know a lot of guys before Doug?

MARAYA. Oh yeah, a lot. Well, a medium lot. I mean compared to some of my friends it wasn't hardly any, but compared to some of my other friends it was more than them.

SUSAN. Was it strange at first? Being with just one guy?

MARAYA. Well, I like Doug, you know. I mean he's not the easiest guy in the world, but then again he says I'm not all that great either. I guess it's how you look at it.

SUSAN. But did you? . . . Like we decided we'd get this place together, right, but then when I thought about it . . . I don't know, you go through this whole number in your head, like are you really ready for this? Is this what you really want? . . .

MARAYA. Try it out. What can you lose. You know, if it doesn't work, you split.

SUSAN. No, what I mean is . . . I thought this was supposed to happen a lot later . . . living with some-one. You know how there's things you're gonna do now

and things you're gonna do later and living with someone was definitely supposed to be a later. But now I
feel like really O.K. about it. I want to try it.

MARAYA. So tell him.

SUSAN. I already have. After five times. He always
says 'yeah, great' and then he never does anything
about it. I remember this one week I even left news-
papers around his apartment, you know, open to the
classifieds . . . apartments for rent. Really. You see
yourself doing this stuff and you don't believe it's you.
And like now, we're travelling around meeting all of
his friends, right? And everyone wants to know where
it's at with us and it's weird because I just don't know.
I don't know. And I don't want to keep pushing him,
either. I always hate it when people do that to me. I
mean that's one of the things I really like about Paul.
He always knows when to back off, but sometimes he's
like so blasé you just want to strangle him. Shit. Listen
to me. I'm making it sound like some kind of big deal.
I don't even know why I brought it up.

MARAYA. That's O.K. Look, I'll tell you how I think
about it. If you want something you ask for it. The
worst thing that can happen is the guy says no and I'm
used to that so it's O.K. and then sometimes he says
yes and then you feel really good.

SUSAN. Don't say anything to Paul, O.K.?

MARAYA. My lips are sealed. Hey, Jakey-poo, you
like that, don't you? That's nice, yes, nice. You can
always tell when he's enjoying it from how he sucks.
It's funny, it even turns me on sometimes. Really. I
love sex. Sometimes when I real depressed I think "how
bad can it be if there's still sex?" (*Truck motor cough-
ing to life Offstage.*) Yea truck! They got the truck
started, honey. Go "Yea truck!" He could care less.
Are you O.K.?

SUSAN. Sure. (*Goes back to loading camera.*)

PAUL. (*Returns, sweaty.*) O.K., who's for the water-fall? I gotta cool off.

MARAYA. Do you have a cigarette? (PAUL *gets them out. Lights one for* MARAYA.) . . . Phew, Jake, you really stink. I swear, sometimes I think this kid borrows shit from somewhere. We don't feed him half of what comes out of him.

SUSAN. You want to come to the waterfall?

MARAYA. Can you just wait while I change the baby . . . maybe I better just put him to bed. Maybe I'll catch up with you later. (MARAYA *starts Off.*)

PAUL. Hey, your cigarette.

MARAYA. Oh, thanks. I gotta stop, I really do. (MARAYA *exits into trailer, puffing.*)

PAUL. You ready?

SUSAN. Sure.

PAUL. O.K., let's go. (SUSAN *gets up, points camera somewhere.*) Susan . . .

SUSAN. What?

PAUL. I want to talk.

SUSAN. Stay like that for a second. C'mon, don't look so serious. We'll talk at the waterfall. (SUSAN *takes a few shots.*) O.K., let's go. (*Exits. Off.*) You coming? (PAUL *looks after her, follows. Fade.*)

SCENE 3

Slide: 1973. Back yard of PAUL *and* SUSAN'S *apartment house. Children's swing and wrought-iron filigree table and chairs painted white but rusting. Low picket fence and gate.* SUSAN *organizes masses of small photos into rows on 4x8 panel which lies flat on the wrought-iron table. One complete board leans against frame of swing. Transistor cassette on ground plays Shubert's Trout Quintet, 3rd*

Movement, Scherzo. Hold on SUSAN *at work for a moment. Then, through gate, enter* BEN BAUMER, *36, in seersucker suit, jacket over shoulder, tie undone, paper bag in one hand. He stops and watches for a moment.*

BEN. Susan?

SUSAN. Hi. You found us.

BEN. Oh yeah. You give a mean set of directions. Didn't get lost once. I'm parked right in front, is that O.K.?

SUSAN. Sure. Hang on a second. (SUSAN *turns off the cassette.*) So. You're Ben.

BEN. Always was, always will be.

SUSAN. Well, it's nice to meet you at last.

BEN. Same to you. And everything you've heard about me is true.

SUSAN. I was expecting a moustache.

BEN. Oh, that. Shaved it off years ago. Paul told you about the moustache, eh?

SUSAN. No, in the picture.

BEN. No kidding. Funny, I don't remember any pictures with a moustache. I only had it a few months.

SUSAN. It's three couples on a beach.

BEN. Oh, God, no. Not the naked one.

SUSAN. It's a great picture. We put it on the bureau.

BEN. Well, god darn! That little so and so! Wouldn't you know it. I have a hundred great pictures of myself and wouldn't you know he'd pick that one. What can you do? The whole family's crazy. Say, where is the little stinker anyway?

SUSAN. Who? Oh, you mean Paul. He's still at the editing room.

BEN. Editing room? What's that all about?

SUSAN. He's editing film. Well, he's learning.

BEN. I thought he was teaching.

SUSAN. He was. Now he's editing film.

BEN. You're trying to tell me he's editing film, right?

SUSAN. Right.

BEN. Well, you live and learn. He never said anything about it.

SUSAN. Can I get you anything . . . beer, coke . . .

BEN. Leave the liquid refreshments to me. (BEN *takes champagne and paper cups from bag.*)

SUSAN. What's that for?

BEN. Celebrazzione.

SUSAN. Shouldn't we wait for Paul?

BEN. No, I got some cheap stuff for him. This is for us. The real thing, a little Dom Pergweenon. Chilled. Just got it in Cambridge.

SUSAN. What's the occasion?

BEN. Hahahaha. Just you wait, Mrs. Higgins, just you wait. (*Twists cork.*) Hold your nose and wiggle your toes. (*Cork pops.*) Ahhh, thank you. I needed that. O.K., one for you, one for me, quick, quick . . . waste not want not . . . a little more for you . . . a lot more for me . . . perfecto. O.K., here's glue in your shoe. (*They drink.*) I'll tell you something. My little brother is a real so and so. He doesn't deserve a beautiful girl like you, and that's my humble opinion. I'll tell you what. Why don't you and me catch the next flight to London before he gets home?

SUSAN. Why London?

BEN. I thought you'd never ask. I got the job.

SUSAN. Oh.

BEN. The job. The London job. He told you about the job, didn't he?

SUSAN. I don't think so.

BEN. He didn't mention anything about . . .

SUSAN. He probably just forgot to tell me. We've had a lot of stuff going on.

BEN. Yeah. Well I guess it's just not that important.

Can't imagine how I got excited about it in the first place.

SUSAN. What is it? Tell me.

BEN. It's only a little matter of opening a multi-million dollar European operation which I'm in charge of. In fact, I created the idea. He did tell you I was in securities?

SUSAN. He said you were a salesman.

BEN. Near enough. Refill?

SUSAN. I'm fine.

BEN. (*Pours for himself.*) No, you see Randle & Lane, that's my company, they've been kind of conservative on overseas markets so I doped out a whole campaign, did a little presentation and they liked it. They liked it a lot. So now I'm in charge of setting the whole thing up. Europe.

SUSAN. That sounds fantastic.

BEN. Listen to this. Sixty thousand a year basic plus commissions. Free car. Six week vacation a year. Five room apartment overlooking jolly old Hyde Park. And the girls in London! I mean talk about yummy! All you want to do is tear the wrappers off and lick 'em to death, I swear.

SUSAN. Aren't you married?

BEN. Yep. Ten years. Great lady, the best. (*Drains cup.*) Little more?

SUSAN. I'm O.K.

BEN. (*Pours for himself. Looks at* SUSAN's *work.*) What's all this?

SUSAN. You like it?

BEN. Very nice. Very nice.

SUSAN. I'm serious. Do you really like it?

BEN. Absolutely. It's . . . different. You work for a photographer?

SUSAN. I *am* a photographer.

BEN. Oh, I'll be darned. So this is your stuff, huh?

What do you sell it or is it a sort of a hobby or what?

SUSAN. I've sold a few. I might be having an exhibit next month. There's a guy that's interested. Just local but . . . gotta start somewhere.

PAUL. (*Voice. Off, as from second floor window.*) What's going on out there?

BEN. Hey, guy . . .

SUSAN. Hi, sweetie.

BEN. Get your rusty butt down here.

PAUL. (*Off.*) Be right down.

SUSAN. (*Pause.*) Listen, congratulations on the job.

BEN. Oh, thank you. Thank you very much. And, ah, fingers crossed for your exhibit. And you never know the way things catch on. There was that movie a couple years ago about surfing. A guy just went out and took a lot of film, just people surfing. Darn movie made him a fortune. You never know. (PAUL *enters through gate.*)

PAUL. Hi Ben.

BEN. Hey, guy, look at you. (*They stand awkwardly.*) You're just in time for a little warm champagne.

PAUL. (*Kisses* SUSAN *hello.*) Hi, babe, how's it going?

SUSAN. O.K. The panel . . .

PAUL. Looks good.

SUSAN. It's coming. You're back early.

(*Enter through gate* SELINA, *very beautiful Chinese-American. Totally American manner and accent.*)

PAUL. Yeah, the lab fucked up the film again so there's nothing to edit. They gave us the afternoon off. (BEN *is watching* SELINA.)

BEN. Can I help you?

SUSAN. Hi Soolie . . .

PAUL. Oh, Selina, this is my brother Ben. This is Selina. She works in the editing room.

BEN. Ah, so that's why he stopped teaching.

SELINA. Excuse me?

PAUL. Soolie wanted to see some of the panels.

SELINA. I didn't know you had company. I'll stop by tomorrow.

SUSAN. Why don't you stay for dinner? Please. I want to show you one of the panels. It still doesn't feel right.

SELINA. How many panels are you going to have?

SUSAN. Twenty I think.

SELINA. Twenty, wow.

SUSAN. Well, I have like over a thousand pictures, right? I set the timer for once every fifteen seconds and the wedding was about nine hours. Figure it out.

BEN. (*At panel.*) This is a wedding? I thought it was one of those you know, what do you call it . . . a happening . . .

SELINA. It was beautiful. That farm is perfect. If they ever want to sell it, let me know. I really love New Hampshire. Listen, I was thinking, you know, you could maybe try a series with the camera going around in a circle. You know. Time the shutter to the motor and you'd see the background changing a little in each picture.

SUSAN. I've thought about that, but I really like it to be one background—just one space and everything that happens in it so you have a reference point. You know, Space Portrait. That's what it is. A portrait of one space.

SELINA. You could call it Circular Space Portrait. I don't know. I was just thinking.

PAUL. Can I say something?

SUSAN. What?

PAUL. You're going up? With Soolie? To look at a panel?

SUSAN. Yeah.

PAUL. If you find yourself anywhere near the fridge . . .

SUSAN. Two beers?

BEN. What? Oh, sure. (SUSAN *and* SELINA *start to go*.)

SELINA. (*To* BEN.) Nice to meet you.

BEN. Well, I hope there's more to come.

SELINA. Excuse me?

PAUL. Never mind. (SUSAN *and* SELINA *exit, talking*.)

SELINA. Avra's really sorry she missed the wedding. She has this great present for you guys. She wants to know when she can come over with it . . .

SUSAN. What is it?

SELINA. She made me promise not to tell. (*They are gone*.)

PAUL. So, d'you drive up?

BEN. Wait a minute. Wait just a minute. I probably heard this wrong. Did that Oriental sweetie pie say something about a present for you? A wedding present?

PAUL. Oh, yeah, Avra. She wanted to watch Watergate so she missed the wedding. Avra's really strange.

BEN. Whose wedding?

PAUL. I was coming to that.

BEN. You're married?

PAUL. Yeah.

BEN. Well, surprise, surprise. When did this happen?

PAUL. Last weekend.

BEN. Gee, guy, excuse me for being a little surprised, here. I mean I talked to Mom on the phone yesterday and she didn't say anything about it. I suppose you didn't tell her, either.

PAUL. Not yet.

BEN. Jesus Christ, Paul, what is it with you?

PAUL. Is this going to be a lecture?

BEN. But your own mother.

PAUL. Did you tell Mom about you and Marlene

splitting up? Did you tell her Marlene had enough of
your drinking and fucking around and doesn't want to
come to London with you if you get that job?

BEN. I got it.

PAUL. Congratulations. Did you tell Mom?

BEN. Of course I told her. I told her the moment I
knew.

PAUL. But you didn't tell her about Marlene. Gee,
Ben, are you trying to keep things from Mom?

BEN. Don't be a wise-ass.

PAUL. All right, then, don't start in about our duties
to Mom. I'm not interested in this game you're trying
to play about the two wonderboys living a great life,
making their little fortunes, raising happy little
families. What's the point? She's sitting there in Seattle
bleeding Dad for all he alimony she can and dumping
it into that ridiculous Ecole de Beauté she runs. I mean,
come on, Ben. What's that got to do with my life?

BEN. I don't get it. Same family, same house, but I
swear to God there's Chinamen I understand better
than I understand you.

PAUL. I noticed. Look. Me and Susan . . . we've
been together for like two years . . . more. It's working out real good, so . . . and if we pay joint taxes it'll
be better for both of us and . . . well she needed to
get a lot of people together for this Space Portrait she
had in mind and we thought a wedding was a great
idea. And we happen to love each other. So. And we
didn't really dig the idea of a lot of relatives crying
their ass off at the beauty of it all and shoving Waring
blenders and matched dinnerware down our throat,
that's all. O.K.?

BEN. No, it's not O.K. because that's not what I'm
talking about and you know it.

PAUL. (*Exploding.*) How the fuck am I supposed to
know what you're talking about? I haven't seen you for

three years and I never understood you back then anyway. I just told you why I got married and why I
didn't tell Mother. Now if that isn't what we're talking
about, suppose you tell me just what the fuck we are
talking about.

BEN. O.K., let's calm down.

PAUL. I'm calm. I'm calm. What? Tell me. What are
we talking about?

BEN. Look. I know what you're going to say, but
just listen to me and let me finish, O.K. I'm going to
have a lot of contacts with this job, very important
contacts . . .

PAUL. Forget it . . .

BEN. Just shut up a second. You've got fantastic
qualifications . . . your background in the Peace Corps,
your honors in college. They look at that resume and
it looks good. It looks real good and then they get to
these years and what do they see? A little teaching
here, a little what is it? Film editing . . . a little of
that . . . And they want to know what was going on.
Believe me, Paul, you can go anywhere you want from
here, but you can't keep faffing around forever.

PAUL. Well, then I'd just better get my act together
lickety-split or I'll miss my golden opportunity to sell
securities, whatever they are.

BEN. I'm not talking about selling securities. I'm
talking about diplomatic work, travel, foreign relations,
all the stuff you were interested in in college.

PAUL. That was a long time ago.

BEN. O.K., look, Paul, I understand, you're going
through something.

PAUL. Oh. What am I going through?

BEN. Well, don't ask me for Christ sake, that's what
I'd like to know. That's what we'd all like to know.

PAUL. All? Suddenly I'm so important. But what am
I going through? You said you understood that I was

going through something and I was just real curious
to know what that was because I keep thinking of it
as my life, but you seem to be anxious for me to get
over it or through it or whatever.

BEN. I'm talking about . . .

PAUL. I know what you're talking about, but your
arrogance just, I don't know, I just can't believe it
sometimes. You come to me with your life in a sham-
bles . . . oh, oh yeah, I know you got a great new job,
but I'm not talking about your job. I'm talking about
your life, Big Ben, your life. I have a little job. I like
it. I know it doesn't take full advantage of my fluency
in Nglene, I know it might raise questions about whatever happened to somebody or other everybody seems
to have thought I was, but that's . . . never mind. The
point is, I'm happy. I have food in the ice box. When
I'm hungry I go there and eat. I have a little money in
the bank. Not too much, but enough; and it's more
than many. There's someone in bed next to me. I'm not
lonely. That's my life, Ben, that's all I want, just a
home, Susan, some kids, just what I can see and touch.
Do you understand what I'm saying? All the other
stuff was and is and will be bullshit forever and ever-
more, amen. I'm happy. And this seems to worry you.

BEN. I'm not worried. I didn't say I was worried.

PAUL. Good for you.

BEN. Look, what are we fighting for? I haven't seen
you for four years. Truce, huh? What do you say?
Let me buy you guys dinner. We'll go out to the snaz-
ziest goddamn restaur . . .

PAUL. Susan's cooking.

BEN. Come on, give the little lady a break, huh?
What do you say? My treat . . .

PAUL. We got food in. Some friends are coming
over. We planned a big dinner for you. You don't have
to impress us, Ben.

BEN. (*Takes a swig of champagne.*) It's not final you know. Me and Marlene. We're taking a year to think it over. There's the kids. (BEN *pours himself more champagne.*)

PAUL. Why don't you hold off on that stuff 'til dinner. We got some nice wine.

BEN. What this? This is nothing. Carbonated French piss. So you're married.

PAUL. Yep.

BEN. Damn. (*Long pause.*) Hey, how come there aren't ice cubes in Poland?

PAUL. Oh, jesus, Ben not now.

BEN. No, this is a good one. You know why?

PAUL. Why?

BEN. I thought you'd never ask. The lady with the recipe died. (BEN *laughs.* PAUL *laughs sadly at* BEN. BEN *thinks he's got* PAUL *with him.*) The lady died . . . dumb, huh? O.K., there's this convention of astronauts . . . this is a quickie . . . they're from all over the world . . . (SUSAN *enters with two beers. Gives* BEN *one.*) Thank you little milkmaid.

SUSAN. (*Walking away.*) It's beer.

BEN. What? Oh, oh, so it is, so it is. Well then, thank you little beermaid . . . (SUSAN *hands* PAUL *beer and starts out.*)

PAUL. Hey.

SUSAN. What?

PAUL. Come here. (SUSAN *does.*) What's going on up there?

SUSAN. Soolie's making a call. I'm just starting dinner.

PAUL. Want a hand?

SUSAN. It's all under control. She's just calling the gallery.

PAUL. O.K. (SUSAN *starts out.*) Wait a minute. What do you mean she's calling the gallery?

SUSAN. She knows the guy. I mean like real well. She's gonna get him to come over later. She thinks he'll give me my own show when he sees the new stuff.

PAUL. Serious?

SUSAN. Yeah.

PAUL. Well, I mean, how come you're so calm? Isn't this sort of woopie-hooray-fucking incredible?

SUSAN. Yeah. I'm a genius. I gotta start the potatoes.

PAUL. Babe! (*They embrace, kiss.* BEN *stands awkwardly, wanders. Blackout.*)

SCENE 4

Slide: 1974. PAUL *and* SUSAN's *living room. Easy chair. Couch. Worn Indian rug. Bricks 'n' boards bookcase. On couch sits* JANICE *and* RUSSELL. *They wear loose fitting Indian mystic style garments.* PAUL *sits in easy chair, a pile of papers by his feet.*

JANICE. Remember, this is a dream I'm talking about. Russell dreamed this. Anyway, then what was it? The girl climbed on the back of this huge white bird . . .

RUSSELL. . . . swan . . .

JANICE. What?

RUSSELL. Swan.

JANICE. Oh yeah right. The bird was a swan and he described this girl and it was a perfect description of Susan who he's never seen a picture of, O.K.? But every detail. And that was on Sunday night which was the same night you said Susan flew to New York. Now, I think that's more than a coincidence.

PAUL. She didn't fly. She took a Greyhound bus.

JANICE. Oh, I thought you said she flew.

RUSSELL. Swan. Greyhound. Animals. Travel. Animals carrying people to new places.

JANICE. And here's the amazing part. The swan put her down and she took out all these pictures out of a case she was carrying and started putting them up on these tall tall buildings and you say Susan's in New York putting up an exhibition of her photography. Russell dreamed this.

PAUL. You sure you don't want a beer or something?

RUSSELL. No alcohol.

PAUL. Oh yeah, I forgot.

RUSSELL. We'll take food later. Thank you.

JANICE. No, but you see what I mean?

PAUL. Well, I'm sorry she's not here.

RUSSELL. No problem. (*They sit for a moment.*)

PAUL. If you say you might pass through New York I could give you her number there. You did say you might pass through New York, right?

RUSSELL. Yes.

PAUL. O.K. Well, I'll give you her number. I'll write it down. (*Starts writing.*) So, you two met in India, huh?

RUSSELL. Yes.

PAUL. That must've been interesting.

RUSSELL. It was.

PAUL. Was it?

RUSSELL. Yes.

PAUL. How? In what way was it interesting?

RUSSELL. (*Thinks.*) Have you been to India?

PAUL. No.

RUSSELL. You should go.

PAUL. Why?

RUSSELL. Different trip. Very different.

JANICE. We used to have these meetings in the ashram where Master would answer questions and . . . he's read a lot of Western literature and he can explain things in a very clear way. He's very modern in a lot of ways . . .

RUSSELL. He's trained in a very ancient tradition.

JANICE. Yeah, the tradition is ancient. I'm not saying about the tradition. I mean as far as that goes I'm not even sure they know how far back—I mean it's one of the oldest schools, right? But when he explains things you just feel he's talking to you, right now, today. Don't you think so, Russ?

RUSSELL. Yes.

JANICE. Yeah you see, that's really what I mean, like even outside the meetings there was this incredible energy everywhere in the ashram—all kinds of different energy at different levels, spiritual, psychic, sexual, oh but let me give you example of the kind of stuff Master could get into. Like remember I told you that . . . oh, I didn't tell you this, O.K., they had this war India and Pakistan, about something and Master made the whole ashram, all the buildings and everything, he made it invisible from the air so the bombers couldn't see where . . .

RUSSELL. Jan. (JANICE *stops immediately.*) Certain times, certain ideas.

JANICE. I was only. I just meant . . . (RUSSELL *smiles.* JANICE *smiles back weakly.* RUSSELL *takes her hand. She is reassured.*)

PAUL. Here's the number.

(*Enter* SELINA *from the kitchen.*)

SELINA. I can't find that pole thing for the middle of the coffee pot.

PAUL. I'll get it. (PAUL *exits into kitchen.* SELINA *sits. Pause.*)

JANICE. So what's the film about? Paul said you and him were working on a script while Susan's in New York.

SELINA. We work on it while she's here too. Where do you know Susan from?

JANICE. We grew up together. We travelled around the world. We're like best friends.

SELINA. Oh, right, you're the one that bought the fish in Bali.

JANICE. (*To* RUSSELL.) We can stop in New York, can't we? All we need to do is change the tickets to New York/Tokyo.

RUSSELL. It could happen.

SELINA. You're going to Tokyo?

RUSSELL. Tokyo, Singapore, Agadir, Cologne, Paris, Leeds, New York again. Circles.

SELINA. You travel a lot, huh?

RUSSELL. Master can't be everywhere. The physical things. Someone has to check them.

SELINA. That's what you do? You check things for this guy Master?

RUSSELL. Master checks. I'm just there.

SELINA. What does he check?

RUSSELL. Everything. Anything.

SELINA. Covers a lot, huh?

RUSSELL. Really.

JANICE. What's the film about?

SELINA. The American Revolution.

RUSSELL. Heavy topic. Historical.

SELINA. It's mainly about this whorehouse in Concord where the British army used to get laid. The producers want to make kind of a porno-musical. We can't figure out if they're crazy or incredibly smart. They used to sell dope and write children's books. They keep their money in this old ice box. Big piles of it. Very weird. Anyway, I guess with the Bicenten-

nial coming up they figure they can cash in if they
get the film out in time.

(*Enter* PAUL *from kitchen carrying tray of cookies.*)

PAUL. Who's that, Ira and Nick?

SELINA. Yeah. D'you find it?

PAUL. It's perking away.

RUSSELL. (*Stands abruptly.*) Thank you.

PAUL. What?

JANICE. We're going? O.K. Well, I guess we'll see
Susan in New York. Anything you want us to take
her?

PAUL. No, that's O.K.

JANICE. Is everything all right?

PAUL. Fine. Fine.

JANICE. O.K. (JANICE *and* RUSSELL *exit.* PAUL *picks
up pages from floor.*)

PAUL. So. Where were we?

SELINA. Do you feel like working?

PAUL. Sure. Why not?

SELINA. You seem distracted.

PAUL. I'm fine. I wasn't expecting company.

SELINA. You were out of it even before they came.

PAUL. No, it was just Janice. I knew what she was
thinking . . . Susan in New York . . . you and me
here. I mean, you can't say anything.

SELINA. O.K., let's work.

PAUL. You're right, I am out of it. She's only been
in New York for five days and already I feel like a
fucking basket case. You know, we haven't been apart
for even a whole day since we started living together.
Three years almost.

SELINA. Call her.

PAUL. She's probably still at the gallery.

SELINA. So call her there.

PAUL. She didn't leave the number.

SELINA. You know the name of the place. Call New York information.

PAUL. Soolie, she doesn't want me to call her there or she'd've given me the number. That's code for 'this is my space, do not invade.'

SELINA. You guys are so weird sometimes.

PAUL. Let's just work on the script.

SELINA. We'll get a lot done, I can tell.

PAUL. (*Opens binder. Stops.*) She was out last night when I called. We usually talk at 11. She wasn't there. She wasn't there all night. She never called.

SELINA. Look, if she was hurt or she got into some kind of trouble somebody'd've called you, don't worry.

PAUL. That's not what I was thinking exactly.

SELINA. You think she's fucking around?

PAUL. I don't know.

SELINA. What would you do if she was?

PAUL. How should I know?

SELINA. If I was in love with a guy and I found out he was doing something like that to me I know what I'd do.

PAUL. What would you do?

SELINA. I'd kill him.

PAUL. We've always had this kind of an understanding, not like a formal thing. Just we picked it up talking to each other, that it'd be all right if we . . . in theory, that is, in theory it was O.K. If we . . . we weren't like exclusively tied down to each other, you know. If we were attracted to someone . . . and we didn't have to necessarily tell each other if we ever . . . unless we were afraid it was getting out of hand . . . like it was getting too serious and we couldn't handle it. But the thing is, we've never been unfaithful. Unfaithful. Funny how it comes back to words like that. We haven't slept with other people. At least I haven't. And I don't think she has except of course there's no way to know for sure since we said we didn't necessarily have to tell each other. But I really don't think she has. She's probably wanted to. I mean I've wanted to so it stands to reason that she's probably wanted to and the fact that she hasn't, or probably hasn't, uncool though it is to admit it, the fact that there's probably this thing she's wanted to do but didn't do it because she knew how it'd make me feel . . . that always made me feel, like admire her. Not admire exactly. Maybe trust. Respect. Trust. Something like that. Some combination of those things.

SELINA. I know what you mean.

PAUL. Yeah, but now that I don't know where she was last night I've been feeling pretty ridiculous, you know. Kind of foolish. Stupid, I don't know what. I was awake all last night thinking about it. I mean, here I am all this time . . . I've known you for what, two years and all that time I've found you like very very attractive, but so what? That's how it goes and now if she's just gone and slept with someone what was all this about? All this holding back for the sake of someone else's feelings . . . and the most ridiculous thing of all is maybe she was in New York thinking you and me were getting it on behind her back and that's what made her . . . if in fact she did do anything, maybe she did it to get even. Or maybe she hasn't done anything. In which case where was she? And why didn't she call?

SELINA. Do you want to sleep with me? Is that what you're saying?

PAUL. No, no that's not what I'm saying. I mean, I have wanted to but that's not the point. Primarily. Although I did say it, didn't I? But I always assumed you sort of . . . it was just one of those things. Have you ever thought about it?

SELINA. Yes, of course.

PAUL. Well. How do you feel about that?

SELINA. About the fact that people are attracted to each other?

PAUL. Have you wanted to sleep with me?

SELINA. I've wanted to do a lot of things I wouldn't do.

PAUL. So you have wanted to. But you wouldn't.

SELINA. If Susan had been in last night, would you?

PAUL. I wish I hadn't brought this up.

SELINA. I think it was a good idea. Bringing it up, I mean. I smell coffee. (SELINA *exits to kitchen.*)

PAUL. (*Calling.*) Selina?

SELINA. (*Off.*) What?

PAUL. Thank you.

SELINA. (*Off.*) You're welcome.

(PAUL *takes script, lies on couch, glances at a few pages. Pause. He lays script aside, can't concentrate. Enter* SUSAN *slowly. Carries small bag. She watches* PAUL *for a moment.*)

SUSAN. Paul.

PAUL. (*Sits up.*) What happened? Why are you back?

SUSAN. Nothing happened. I took the day off. Are you working?

PAUL. Where were you last night?

SUSAN. I stayed with a friend. Are you glad to see me?

PAUL. Susan. (PAUL *and* SUSAN *embrace.* SELINA *appears with two cups of coffee. Stands for a moment.*) You didn't call. I was worried.

SUSAN. I was going to. I'm sorry.

PAUL. Why didn't you? (SELINA *withdraws into kitchen.*)

SUSAN. I was here.

PAUL. Where? In Boston?

SUSAN. Yeah.

PAUL. Last night?

SUSAN. Paul, I have to tell you something.

PAUL. Oh shit. What is it?

SUSAN. I stayed with Katie last night.

PAUL. Katie. Katie Moffatt? That's downstairs. You stayed downstairs? You came up from New York and you stayed downstairs?

SUSAN. Let me tell you what happened.

PAUL. Yeah, why don't you do that.

SUSAN. I came up. I flew up. I wanted to surprise you. And then at the airport I just . . . I don't know. I just got angry that I'd come all this way because I missed you. I was gonna call. I was going to pretend I was still in New York, but then, I don't know . . . I didn't.

PAUL. I noticed.

SUSAN. Paul, I'm sorry, I'm trying to explain. I mean I don't feel wonderful about this. In fact, I feel pretty damn stupid. I know it was a dumb thing to do and I felt even worse when I realized why I'd . . . I wanted you to worry. I wanted that. I know it's shitty, but I wanted to get back at you for making me come all the way up to Boston when I should be working on the show . . . Yeah, I know. I just have to tell you that. What I'm trying to say is . . . I seem to have this little problem accepting the fact that I . . . I'm just so fucking in love with you, Paul. That's all it is, and I can't stand being away from you. (SUSAN *controlling herself.* PAUL *comes to her. They embrace.* SUSAN *weepy.*)

PAUL. Hey. Hey. (*They kiss. Passionately.* SELINA *comes back. Stands. Fade.*)

Scene 5

*Slide: 1975. Central Park. Afternoon. Benches and
garbage can. PAUL, SUSAN and MARAYA eat from
"family size" bucket of Kentucky Fried Chicken.
PAUL holds BABY-MATTY while MARAYA prepares
a bottle. MARAYA is pregnant.*

MARAYA. I don't know. I guess he was just pissed
off about something. I don't even remember what it
was any more, but he picked up this big ole kitchen
knife and slammed it into the table. Went in about an
inch and that table's solid oak. I mean he was really
mad. (*To* BABY-MATTY.) I'm just telling about daddy,
honey. Don't worry, everything's O.K. (MARAYA *gives
bottle to* PAUL *who feeds* BABY-MATTY.)

SUSAN. But how'd he hurt his hand?

MARAYA. Oh, he wasn't holding the handle tight
enough. It slipped down over the blade.

SUSAN. Yech!

MARAYA. Really. Poor Doug. Twenty-three stitches.
He's O.K. now, but he has to take these pain killers
and that could be a drag in the interview 'cause these
pills are like super zappo strong and they make you
really high. And they don't kill the pain, either.

PAUL. (*Looks at* SUSAN's *watch.*) It's ten past one.

MARAYA. (*Yelling.*) DOUG!! (*To* BABY-MATTY.)
Sorry, honey, I was just calling daddy.

(*Enter* DOUG *looking back over his shoulder. He has
a huge bandage-wrap and position brace on right
hand. Dog barks, Off.*)

DOUG. You heard what I said, Jake. Stay away
from that doggie. Hey, man I'm serious. I'll punch
your fucking head in.

MARAYA. Doug, don't talk to him like that. He can play with the dog. It's not gonna hurt him.

DOUG. Yeah and when it bites him and he gets rabies who's gonna pay the hospital bills?

PAUL. It's ten past, Doug. It'll take you a good half hour to get down to Wall Street from here.

SUSAN. It takes fifteen minutes.

DOUG. I gotta have a joint. Where's your purse, Marsie?

MARAYA. You can't get stoned now, honey. You're going to see the president of a bank.

DOUG. Fuck him. Man, my hand hurts. If he doesn't want to lend me the bread, I'll get it someplace else.

MARAYA. Doug, you're talking about five hundred thousand dollars. Another bank wouldn't let you in the door. (*To* SUSAN.) The president is Cisco's uncle.

DOUG. What do you know about it anyway? Man, if I can't get a few bucks from some sucker unless he's my buddy's uncle I don't even want it.

MARAYA. He's not just your buddy—he's your partner.

DOUG. Some fucking partner. If I didn't do all the work myself we'd finish about one house a century. Come on, where's the dope?

MARAYA. No, Doug, you can't have it.

DOUG. My hand's killing me. I can't think straight. (*Dog barks, Off.*)

MARAYA. No.

DOUG. (*Yelling.*) Jake, what'd I tell you about that doggie? Leave him alone or I'm gonna hurt you. If you want to stay over there . . . (*Barking stops.*) O.K., that's better.

SUSAN. He's cute.

DOUG. I'll tell you one thing. If I get this bread I'm gonna buy Cisco out and run the business myself, unless you want to come in with me.

PAUL. Me?

DOUG. You never think I'm being serious. Man, I mean it. You don't know some of the shit I'm getting into. I'm gonna be a rich man. That guy I built the house for, you remember him. Mr. Conklin, the guy with the big lump on his neck? Well, he was real pleased with my work—read pleased. And he bought this big ole chunk of prime lakefront property and when he found out I was with the 23rd tactical in Nam . . . that was his outfit in the second world war . . . that did it, man. Got the contract just like that. Fourteen houses. You know what that'll be worth?

MARAYA. Doug, you haven't even got the money yet.

DOUG. Listen, man, with this deal going any bank that ain't standing in line to lend me the bread is a bank with its head up its ass. One joint, Marsie, huh?

MARAYA. No.

DOUG. One toke. One fucking toke is all.

MARAYA. No, Doug, you can't.

PAUL. (*Looks at* SUSAN's *watch.*) It's twenty past.

MARAYA. We better get moving.

DOUG. Yeah, O.K. (*Yells.*) Hey, Jake, come on, kid, it's bank time. Man, I'll tell ya, I'm no good at this shit. I'm just not. I don't know why the fuck Cisco can't take care of it. It's his uncle.

SUSAN. Why doesn't he?

DOUG. He doesn't have a suit. Naa, I don't know. JAKE! He hates his uncle. In fact, I think it's mutual, but I'm supposed to promise this dude Cisco'll straighten out if he lends us the bread. The family's impressed that Cisco's a partner in a company. Shit-kicker Construction Unlimited. I'll tell you what I can't figure out is how anyone'd think it's worth half a million to get Cisco right. I like the dude. He's my partner and I'll carry him through a lot of shit for sure, but Cisco, man, you could get him straight as a ruler and I still wouldn't pay you more'n a dollar for him.

MARAYA. Are we going or not?

DOUG. Yeah, yeah, we're going. This is weird. This is definitely non-normal. I gotta go talk bullshit to a bank president. Doug Superfreak meets Mr. Straight-money. You guys'll come up, right?

SUSAN. We'll see you soon. Good luck.

DOUG. I don't know how you guys can live in this city. Look at that squirrel. He's got hepatitis, no shit. Look at him. Pathetic. Shooting up with a dirty needle. Give him an hour in the country and he'd forget there ever was a Central Park. You should move up. I'm serious. I dump Cisco, we go 50-50 on the business, you bring you camera, take pictures of trees and shit like that. It's so pretty up there.

MARAYA. Doug.

DOUG. O.K., O.K., take it easy. See you guys. Hey, Jakie-poo. (*Exits.*)

SUSAN. When are you expecting?

PAUL. Susan, they have to go.

MARAYA. November, and that's absolutely the last one. It was a mistake believe me. (*To* BABY-MATTY.) Not you, honey, the next one. All I can tell you is don't listen to doctors. They said I was safe for a couple months after Matty here . . . four weeks later, bang. Four weeks. Oh well, gotta go. You guys take care, huh. (*For* BABY-MATTY.) "Bye-bye. Go "bye-bye." Bye. (*Exits. Pause.* SUSAN *offers some chicken.*)

SUSAN. Want some more?

PAUL. No. (*Pause.*)

SUSAN. How've you been?

PAUL. Great. You?

SUSAN. O.K.

PAUL. So much for the good news.

SUSAN. Did you sell the script yet?

PAUL. No.

SUSAN. It'll happen, don't worry.

PAUL. No it won't. It's a piece of shit.

SUSAN. I read it. I thought it was good.

PAUL. Yet another point of agreement.

SUSAN. Paul, what's the matter?

PAUL. Why'd you have to go invite Doug and Maraya?

SUSAN. I thought you'd want to see them. They're your friends.

PAUL. But now?

SUSAN. They're only in town for the day. They have to go back this afternoon.

PAUL. Susan, for christ sakes, we haven't seen each other for three months. We do have things to talk about.

SUSAN. I'm sorry. I thought you'd want to see them. We have all afternoon to talk.

PAUL. I thought you had to work.

SUSAN. I can take the afternoon off.

PAUL. Nice job.

SUSAN. Yes, as a matter of fact, it's a very nice job.

PAUL. Taking pictures of rich people's houses.

SUSAN. I knew that's how you'd see it.

PAUL. Sorry.

SUSAN. Paul, it does happen to be the best architectural journal in the country. In fact, it's one of the best in the world. And I like working there. I like the people. I like their ideas. I like what they're trying to do with the magazine and I like the fact that I'm beginning to feel like I can take my work seriously for the first time.

PAUL. I said I'm sorry.

SUSAN. I heard you.

PAUL. Moving right along.

SUSAN. And another thing, Paul. I need to make my

own living. I never realized it before, how much I hated taking money from you, from my family. Now I don't feel like I have to apologize for anything any more and that's important, Paul. You're not the only one around here that's proud, you know.

PAUL. You're right. And I'm sorry. Really. That was stupid. I didn't mean to put you down.

SUSAN. I know you didn't. I just had to tell you. Oh, babe, it's so nice to see you.

PAUL. I miss you.

SUSAN. Well, I miss you too.

PAUL. A lot?

SUSAN. Yeah, pretty much a whole lot.

PAUL. Were you . . . have you been with anyone else?

SUSAN. As in guys? A few. How about you?

PAUL. Guys? Not many.

SUSAN. 'Cause I was with a woman. Once. Life's infinite variety.

PAUL. How interesting. Was it nice?

SUSAN. No. I mean yes, in a way, but no, not really. I miss making love to you.

PAUL. Yeah, that part was always pretty good.

SUSAN. Was? Why do you talk about it like it's over? (*Pause.*) Is it?

PAUL. I don't know, is it?

SUSAN. Isn't that what we're supposed to be talking about? This wasn't supposed to be permanent. I thought we were just trying out a little time on our own. You want to end it?

PAUL. No.

SUSAN. So let's talk about it.

PAUL. That's what we're doing.

SUSAN. O.K. Things are going pretty well for me, you know.

PAUL. So I gathered.

SUSAN. What I mean is, I can't move back to Boston.

PAUL. Can't? You're being physically restrained?

SUSAN. I don't want to.

PAUL. Ah. So I'd have to move to New York, is that it?

SUSAN. You don't have to make it sound like the end of the world. You always talked about moving to New York.

PAUL. I'm just trying to clarify the situation.

SUSAN. You could do so well here, Paul.

PAUL. I'm doing just fine in Boston. All our friends are there. I've been made a full editor. I like it there.

SUSAN. But you said you wanted your own business one day. You can do it here. There's a lot more film happening here than there is in Boston. And I'm meeting a lot of people who might be able to help.

PAUL. You sound like my brother.

SUSAN. Well, what's wrong with getting a little help, for God sake? Soolie helped me. I've helped some people here. It's not just a favor, you know. You do it because you think someone's good. And you are, babe. You should be doing . . . just, something more like what I know you're capable of doing. Why do you keep fighting it?

PAUL. We should have a sex change before we think about getting back together.

SUSAN. Well, you're the one that always said it. "If you're white, middle class and American you have to work 24 hours a day to not make it." So stop working so hard.

PAUL. O.K., let's say I move to New York. That's condition number one, right? So let's say I accept that . . .

SUSAN. Don't do me any favors.

PAUL. Well, for christ sake, that's what you're saying, isn't it? If I want you, I have to have New York.

SUSAN. It isn't a condition.

PAUL. Everything is a condition, Susan. Everything.

SUSAN. What are you saying?

PAUL. I just want to know what I get in exchange.

SUSAN. What do you want?

PAUL. You know what I want.

SUSAN. Oh.

PAUL. Have you thought about it?

SUSAN. I don't think either of us is ready for that.

PAUL. That's bullshit . . .

SUSAN. I'm not.

PAUL. Well when? We can't start when we're sixty.

SUSAN. I'm thirty one.

PAUL. Great. Only twenty-nine years to go.

SUSAN. Would you want to be our child, Paul? I mean honestly, at this point in time do you really think you'd want to have the two of us for parents?

PAUL. We're no worse than a few I grew up with.

SUSAN. That's what I mean. I want to have kids someday. I do. Just not now.

PAUL. So what's the score so far? Paul moves to New York. Susan remains childless. That's two to nothing. I need some points here.

SUSAN. We'll talk about it, O.K.?

PAUL. We'll talk about it? That sounds familiar.

SUSAN. Well, you can't just expect me to say yeah, great. "You want kids, we'll have kids." It is something we have to talk about.

PAUL. O.K. That's half a point, right?

SUSAN. Can you stay for the weekend? I think we should spend some time together. I'd like you to meet some of my friends. I've bored them to death talking about you. I don't think they believe you exist. There's a party tomorrow night. I have room at my place.

PAUL. Is that an offer?

SUSAN. Can you stay?

PAUL. Yeah.

SUSAN. Good. (*They kiss.*) Let's clear up here.

PAUL. Are we going somewhere?

SUSAN. We can talk at my place.

PAUL. As opposed to here where we can't talk?

SUSAN. You want to stay here?

PAUL. No, I want to go back to your place. And talk.

SUSAN. I'm expecting a call, that's all.

PAUL. Oh.

SUSAN. Come on. (*They rise.*)

PAUL. Susan.

SUSAN. What?

PAUL. What is it? I feel like . . . I don't know.

SUSAN. It's been three months. We need time. Let's go. (*Exits. Off.*) You coming, babe? (PAUL *follows. Fried chicken on bench. Fade.*)

SCENE 6

Slide: 1977. PAUL *and* SUSAN's *living room, Central Park West. Evening. Painter's drop cloth on floor. Ladder, buckets of paint, paint tray brushes. Pile of boxes covered with sheet. Armchair.* SUSAN *and* SELINA *sit on floor finishing take-out Chinese meal. They are in work clothes. As lights go up, they are convulsed with laughter.*

SUSAN. I don't believe it. What's your say?

SELINA. (*Breaks her fortune cookie and reads.*) "He who knows not, but knows not that he knows not is a fool. Shun him." That's a fortune?

SUSAN. Whew. Heavy.

SELINA. Someone at the cookie factory's been working overtime.

*SUSAN. (*Looks into food container.*) Want some more?

SELINA. I'm stuffed.

SUSAN. All in all I'd call that a pretty shitty meal.

SELINA. It's better than I could do.

PAUL. (*Off.*) What time is it?

SUSAN. Ten past.

SELINA. Is he really serious about the job?

SUSAN. Why would he joke about something like that?

SELINA. He's already got two editors working for him. I don't see why he needs me.

SUSAN. 'Cause Bert's a jerk. Paul ought to fire him but he won't so he's gonna need someone else around who really knows what they're doing. Look, it's a big deal. First feature film. He doesn't want to fuck it up.

SELINA. I thought he didn't have it yet. Isn't that why he's going to California?

SUSAN. That's just a formality. He already knows definitely they want him, but there's this whole ritual you have to do . . . meet the director . . . meet the producer . . . sit around for a few days snorting coke. That's how they do business.

SELINA. I've never worked on a feature.

PAUL. (*Off.*) What time is it?

SUSAN. Quarter past. I wish he'd get a watch. Listen, I know you're worried. It's a big move. I mean I was terrified when I came to New York the first time. Remember my show . . . ?

SELINA. The Space Portraits?

SUSAN. Right. Jesus, the things I didn't know about photography. It feels like about a million years ago.

* (The scene can start here if you prefer)

SELINA. I liked the Space Portraits.

SUSAN. Oh, sure, they were O.K., I mean for what I knew then, they were great, but until I met people who really knew what they were doing . . . 'cause if they see you've got something, they'll open right up . . . let you pick their brains, ask questions, tell you what you're doing wrong, show you all the stuff you have to know to get really good and, I mean, that's what it's all about finally. Just, when you can see yourself making real choices in the work and you know they're right, even though you don't know how you know any more. Like now my eye just sees when it's perfect, when it's clear, you know, when it's simple. You know what it is. It's when you finally see a whole pattern under everything and you know exactly how much of it you have to show to suggest the whole thing. Anyway. I'm rambling, aren't I? I keep doing that lately. What were we talking about? Oh yeah, New York.

SELINA. I'll think about it.

SUSAN. Promise?

SELINA. Cross my heart and hope to die.

PAUL. (*Off.*) What time is it?

SUSAN. (*Ignores him.*) 'Cause Paul's really convinced you're one of the best editors he's ever worked with. You taught him for god sake. But who's ever gonna know how good you are when you're stuck up in Boston?

(PAUL *rushes in with small suitcase. He wears a three-piece suit, has moustache, looks trendy.*)

PAUL. Susie, what the hell did I do with my . . . oh, here they are. (*Pats his jacket.*)

SUSAN. What?

PAUL. My joints. I forgot I had 'em. Man, do I

hate flying. Let me have a little vino. What time is it?

SUSAN. Calm down, babe.

PAUL. I'm calm, I'm calm. (*Takes swig from bottle.*) That's better. Well, I guess I'd better get moving.

SUSAN. Can't you wait a few more minutes? He's on his way.

PAUL. Who?

SUSAN. Lawrence.

PAUL. Oh yeah, right. What time is it?

SUSAN. Twenty-two past.

PAUL. I don't want to get caught in traffic. The plane's leaving in 45 minutes.

SUSAN. There won't be any traffic.

PAUL. That's what you said the last time and it took an hour.

SUSAN. Last time wasn't the 4th of July weekend. Everyone's out of town. Calm down.

PAUL. Look, I saw Lawrence a few days ago. Just tell him I had to go. Tell him I'm sorry I missed him. I'm not trying to avoid him. I think he's a wonderful human being. I love the new beds. He has marvelous taste and we'll all have dinner when I get back, O.K.?

SUSAN. You know he's going to be hurt. He thinks you don't like him.

PAUL. He thinks everybody doesn't like him. Now come on. Wish me luck. I have to go.

SUSAN. (*Hugs him.*) Good luck. I'll miss you.

PAUL. I'll call as soon as I get to the hotel. You gonna watch the fireworks from the terrace?

SUSAN. I guess so.

PAUL. I'll tell the pilot to buzz Central Park West and waggle his wings.

SUSAN. O.K., we'll wave.

PAUL. Bye, Soolie. (*They hug.*) You still be here Friday night?

SELINA. I don't know yet.

PAUL. If you're not, I'll call you.

SELINA. Good luck.

PAUL. It's in the bag. Shit, I hate flying. (*Starts out.*)

SUSAN. Hey.

PAUL. What?

SUSAN. What about Bert?

PAUL. What about him?

SUSAN. You're not going to let him do that final cut on the Slumbermax commercial by himself? Come on, babe.

PAUL. I left instructions on the wall. He'll know what to do.

SUSAN. Like he did the last time?

PAUL. What can I do? Everyone else is tied up.

SUSAN. Everyone?

PAUL. Lindzee's busy, Stan's busy, Al's busy, Mike's busy, everyone's busy. (*Pause.* SUSAN *is looking at* SELINA.)

SELINA. Hey, come on, I can't . . .

PAUL. It's a piece of cake, Soolie . . .

SELINA. This is my vacation.

PAUL. You could do it in your sleep. It'll take a day. I've got it all laid out, even the frame counts.

SELINA. You guys are real subtle.

PAUL. Yes?

SELINA. O.K. One day.

PAUL. (*To* SUSAN.) The log book's on top of the film rack. My work sheet's taped to the back of my office door. Warn Bert, by the way. Do you have his number in the country? Can you remember all that?

SUSAN. Logbook, filmrack, work sheet, back of door, warn Bert, country number, twenty-five past.

PAUL. What?

SUSAN. It's twenty-five past.

PAUL. Oh, O.K. Shit. Bye. (*Exits.*)

SUSAN. Thanks.

SELINA. Yeah, good old Soolie. (SUSAN *sits, leans back.*) You feeling O.K.?

SUSAN. Huh? Oh, yeah, I'm fine. I guess I had too much wine or something. Maybe it's the monosodium.

SELINA. Maybe you ought to lie down.

SUSAN. No, I'm O.K. Lawrence'll be here in a minute. I'll be all right.

SELINA. You don't look all right.

SUSAN. Excuse me. (*Rises, starts out. Stops. Breathes deep. Returns. Sits.*) False alarm.

SELINA. Are you pregnant or something?

SUSAN. Yeah.

SELINA. Really?

SUSAN. Really.

SELINA. Paul didn't say anything.

SUSAN. I just found out, and don't say anything until I get a chance to tell him, O.K.?

SELINA. Man, I'd really like to be pregnant right now. I was thinking of just doing it, you know. Since it doesn't look like I'm having too much luck finding a guy I can put up with for more than a day or two. Just get someone to, you know, just contribute. Are you happy?

SUSAN. I don't know. That's the whole problem. I just don't know how I feel. We had all these heavy talks when we got back together. You know—should we have a baby—shouldn't we have a baby and we sort of decided, well, we didn't really decide anything. Just we'd, we wouldn't exactly try, but then again we wouldn't exactly not try and then if something happened we'd deal with it.

SELINA. So something happened.

SUSAN. Yeah, and here I am, dealing with it. You know, I had such an incredible feeling when I got the results of the test. Just . . . there you are, it finally happened. I was like totally serene, just sort of floated home and I had this whole fantasy, you know, all those pregnant women you see walking around with that funny little smile on their face, the big secret . . .

SELINA. . . . and huge tits . . .

SUSAN. God, Paul would love that. Oh, and I got this idea for a series of self portraits all through the pregnancy, the different stages. You could do it with a permanent camera in the bedroom so everything would be the same in the picture except I'd be getting bigger and bigger. But the thing is, when I started thinking about it I realized I was really into the idea of the photographs, but I wasn't really all that into the idea of being pregnant.

SELINA. You don't really want to tell him, do you?

SUSAN. Of course I want to tell him. I mean, O.K. I guess maybe I just want to get comfortable with the idea first so I know how I feel about it. We're the ones who have to do all the work, right?

SELINA. Yeah, I guess.

SUSAN. I don't know. It's just so nice the way things are now and the thing is he hasn't said anything about a baby for like . . . well, ever since the business started doing well. Not one word. So I guess it really was some kind of competitive thing. You know, I get pregnant so I can't work as much and that makes me less of a threat. The old story. Does that make sense?

SELINA. Oh, yeah. It makes sense. Sure.

SUSAN. So what do you think?

SELINA. I don't see why you don't want to tell him. He's doing well, you're doing well. Everything seems to be working out. So what's the problem?

SUSAN. There's no problem.

SELINA. Oh. Then what are we talking about?

SUSAN. (*Pause.*) Why do you always take his side?

SELINA. Who's side?

SUSAN. Whenver I try to talk to you about something you always . . . like, I really thought you'd understand about something like this . . . sisterhood and all that. I mean I have a right to my own thoughts, don't I? It's not so terrible that I don't want to say anything to him until I know for sure how I feel about what my body is going to have to be doing for the next however many months and then when I know for sure I'll tell him about it and that way it won't get all messy with me getting my feelings all tangled up in the way he feels about it until we don't know who feels what about anything anymore, which is what always seems to happen with us. But whenever I try to talk to you I feel like you think I'm being . . . I don't know . . . like you automatically think I'm doing the wrong thing. Well?

SELINA. What are you asking me?

SUSAN. Yeah, you see? Like that kind of remark. What's that supposed to mean? Oh, shit, Soolie, listen to me. I sound like a witch. I'm sorry. I really am sorry. I just, I don't know what to do about this. (*Phone by* SUSAN *rings. She picks up.*) Hello? Yeah, he can come up. (*Hangs up.*) I'm thirty-three. If I don't have it now . . . God, why is everything so fucking complicated? They ought to have a course in making up your mind. I'm sorry, but you see what I mean, don't you?

SELINA. Oh. Sure. You have a problem, that's all. It's O.K. You just have a problem.

SUSAN. I'm glad you think so.

SELINA. I don't really think anything you know. All I think is I'm always in the middle with you two. Paul talks to me. You talk to me. Don't you ever talk to each other? I don't know what you should do. It's not my life. I mean I have enough of my own stuff to figure out and I don't go around asking people what I should do because they're my problems and they're not very interesting unless you're me. In which case, they're mostly just a pain in the ass. I'd like to move to New York, for instance. I'd like to work for Paul. I think I'm probably ready for it although I think there must be a lot of editors around as good as me and that makes me wonder why you want to move here. Is it because I'm good at my job or because you like me or because you and Paul don't know how to deal with each other and you need me as a middle man?

SUSAN. I didn't know you felt that way.

SELINA. You never asked. And I don't always feel that way either.

SUSAN. I think we better straighten this out.

SELINA. O.K. (*Doorbell rings.*)

SUSAN. Shit. I'll be right back. (*Exits.*)

(SELINA *pours more wine. Talking Offstage, then enter* SUSAN *followed by* LAWRENCE, *talking.*)

LAWRENCE. . . . and then in the middle they had this incredible column of balloons right up to the ceiling and out like branches, god, I love balloons. I decided that's what's been missing from my life. I'm going to have balloons in my life. I'm going to just walk around my apartment and kick balloons in front of me. Doesn't that sound fabulous? Just kicking balloons around in your own apartment. Except I'm going to only have one color—just white ones. Too many different colors would just get confusing and who needs more confusion? Hello. I'm Lawrence.

SUSAN. This is Selina.

LAWRENCE. Hi, Selina.

SELINA. Hello.

LAWRENCE. I love your turquoise. Where'd you get it, Arizona?

SELINA. Boston.

LAWRENCE. God, the Navahoes are everywhere. I always wanted a pendant like that. Isn't it funny how everyone's wearing turquoise nowadays? I never used to like it, but now everyone's wearing it and I'm beginning to see what they mean. There's nothing like a trend to change the way you feel about things.

SUSAN. If you want to see how the beds look, they're here.

LAWRENCE. The beds. What beds? Oh, the beds. Did they arrive already?

SUSAN. In the two end rooms. Why don't you have a look.

LAWRENCE. Was this a heavy conversation or something?

SUSAN. Yeah.

LAWRENCE. God, what a 4th of July. I've spent the whole day being rejected by everyone. Sylvia thinks I hate her because I was staring again. I swear I don't know what to do about it. I just can't help it. She's so glamorous for her age all she has to do is start talking to me and all I can do is stare at her and for some reason that makes her think I don't like her. Maybe I stare wrong. Maybe I should learn a new way to stare. Do you have a mirror? I'll practice. Do you like the beds?

SUSAN. Oh, yeah. They're great.

LAWRENCE. Aren't they sensational? I was going to get one for myself, but then I'd have to redo the bedroom and I'm not in the mood. How long is this going to take?

SUSAN. We'll just be a few minutes.

LAWRENCE. All right. Call me when you're done. May I have some wine? (SUSAN *pours him a glass.*)

Maybe I'll watch some TV after I look at the beds.
Do you have a TV guide?

SUSAN. In the bedroom.

LAWRENCE. Where's Paul?

SUSAN. He had to catch a flight.

LAWRENCE. They all say that, don't they? Story of
my life. (*The wine.*) That's some champagne for later.
(*The bag.*) I stole it from Sylvia's party and whatever you do, don't tell her I came here. I said I was
sick. God, I hope she doesn't call my place. I forgot
to take the phone off the hook. It's just her parties
are always the pits. She has fabulous decorations and
terrible company. It's always the same thing. She
just doesn't know who to invite. I mean D minus for
people. This time it was all these horrible On The
Waterfront types. You know the kind—leather jackets
and keys hanging off their jeans. God, I can't wait
till that style goes out. It reminds me of the janitor
at my high school. And the silliest thing is I know
she's doing it for me, but I don't know where she got
the idea I was into leather. I hate it to death. Oh,
and then she stopped me on the way out, Sylvia, did
you ever notice how she does that? Waits till you're
on the way out the door and then she hits you with
some heavy dilemma? Some earth shattering problem? Like this time it was, "should she have a face
lift?" I mean, really. I just had to stand there and
pretend to think about it when I knew she'd already
made up her mind and all she wanted is for me to
agree. That's all anybody ever wants. And then there
I was staring at her again. Yes, I know, you're talking.
I'm sorry. If you'd had the day I just had you'd
understand. Don't be too long. (*Exits towards bedroom.*)

SELINA. Who is he?

SUSAN. My boss. You know, on the magazine. He's

helping us decorate. He found us the beds. Do you feel like talking?

SELINA. I don't have anything to say, really.

SUSAN. You think I should tell Paul?

SELINA. It's up to you.

SUSAN. I don't really feel like talking anymore. Maybe tomorrow. Are you angry?

SELINA. Why should I be angry?

SUSAN. Should I tell Lawrence to come back? Jesus, what do I keep asking you for?

PAUL. (*Rushes in.*) I forgot my fucking ticket. I got all the way to the mid-town tunnel and I realized I didn't have my ticket. I could've sworn I put it in my travel wallet. I put my wallet in my bag . . . Wait a minute. Oh no. I think I might've just done a very dumb thing.

SUSAN. What?

PAUL. (*Opens jacket, looks, closes it quickly.*) I just did a very dumb thing. I have my ticket. My ticket is in my pocket.

SUSAN. Are you stoned?

PAUL. I was on my way to the airport. Of course I'm stoned.

SUSAN. You can still make it. It only takes half an hour.

PAUL. Yeah . . . but I think I don't want to. There seems to be something bigger than all of us telling me to stay.

SUSAN. You have a meeting, babe.

PAUL. Not 'til late tomorrow. I can make it if I catch an early flight and I remember my ticket. Remember that I have my ticket, that is.

LAWRENCE. (*Re-enter.*) Oh, good. I thought I heard something. How was California?

PAUL. Not bad. How was the party?

LAWRENCE. It was just on the verge of complete

catastrophe when I left. Thank god you're here. They banished me to the bedroom with nothing good on TV.

SUSAN. So do you want to try to make the flight or stay and watch the fireworks?

PAUL. Is that champagne?

LAWRENCE. Chateau Sylvia.

PAUL. I'll stay and watch the fireworks.

LAWRENCE. Can I open it? (*Takes out the bottles, opening one.*) Oh, dear, good old America. Two hundred and one years old and looking every minute of it. Actually, I think we should have stopped the whole show last year. I mean two hundred years is enough for any country, don't you think? There's just no way we can go anywhere but downhill after this. Hold your breath. (*Uncorks bottle. No pop. No fizz. Looks into bottle.*) God, and I thought Sylvia was flat. (PAUL *laughs.* LAWRENCE *laughs. Others join. They stop abruptly.*) What are we laughing at?

PAUL. I don't know. (*They laugh again. Fade.*)

SCENE 7

Slide: 1978. Terrace of PAUL *and* SUSAN's *apartment. Deck chairs. Doors to apartment. Portable barbeque. Plants.* SUSAN *and* JANICE *on deck chairs taking the sun.* JANICE *smokes constantly and drinks a beer.*

JANICE. I think it's just a question of respect. Mutual respect.

SUSAN. Yeah.

JANICE. Phil respects me. I respect him. I mean, that's it.

SUSAN. Yeah.

JANICE. Like with Russell, well, you never met him, but believe me . . . O.K. . . . a typical example of

Russell. This time we were in Boston, but you'd gone to New York and I wanted to stop and see you. It was no big deal, real easy to change the tickets, but he wouldn't do it. You know why? Get this. I was too attached to the things of this world. That's what he said. O.K. So one time we were back in San Francisco and he saw this sports car and he bought it. I couldn't believe it. He wasn't even into cars or if he was I never knew about it. I never knew a lot of things about him, but when I said what about the things of this world, I mean, you can go buy a car, but I can't see a friend. You know what he says? He can buy the car because he isn't attached to it. He doesn't need it. Great. And the dumb thing is, I believed him. Like completely. No, not completely. No, that's right, that's what I was starting to say. (*Offers cigarette.*) Want one?

SUSAN. No, I quit.

JANICE. Oh, yeah? When.

SUSAN. Six months ago.

JANICE. Wow. But, you know . . . I really do believe there's this part of you that knows better and all it takes is for one thing to happen. Like with Russell we were meditating one day. Well, he was. I couldn't get into it, so I was just sort of pretending. I did that a lot. That's another thing. I used to wonder if he knew I was pretending, 'cause if he's supposed to be so spiritual he should be able to tell, right? But he never said anything. Anyway, this one time I was telling you about, I just started watching him, sort of squinting, and all of a sudden he like started changing shape in front of me and I could see the pores in his skin and all these little hairs all over his body. It's like he just turned evil right in front of me. I was even thinking later that maybe it was this really ironic thing happening. You know. Like the first time I finally had a mystical insight while I was meditating and what I saw was the guy that had got me into it in the first place, was this really evil creep. Anyway, I just got up and walked out. He was still meditating. I never saw him again. It's weird how these things work out. Oh, by the way, my mother says hi. That's another great thing about being with Phil. I can go home again. I never wanted my folks to meet Russell. Phil and Paul really seem to be hitting it off. Phil usually takes a long time to like people. It's mostly he's just shy, I guess. I remember on our honeymoon we went to the Grand Canyon and he hardly talked to anyone at the hotel. I thought maybe he was angry. He's just shy. Do you like him? Sue. Susie? Susan.

SUSAN. (*Waking.*) Huh? Sorry. What?

JANICE. Do you like Phil?

SUSAN. Who's Phil? Oh, Phil. Yeah. He seems like a nice guy.

JANICE. You guys seem real happy. Paul's in a great mood.

SUSAN. The film went well. They finished editing last month.

JANICE. I never realized he was so like, well, I never really knew him or anything, but he's really lively. Sometimes I'm not sure how to take him. (*Airplane flies over. They watch.*)

SUSAN. Where is everybody?

JANICE. They're inside.

BEN. (*Enters.*) How are the bathing beauties doing out here?

SUSAN. What's going on in there? (*Singing from inside. Enter* PAUL *and* PHIL *with birthday cake.*)

PAUL and PHIL.

HAPPY BIRTHDAY TO YOU

HAPPY BIRTHDAY TO YOU . . .

SUSAN. Oh no!!!

ALL.

HAPPY BIRTHDAY DEAR SUSAN
HAPPY BIRTHDAY TO YOUUUUU!!!!!!

SUSAN. I thought there was something fishy going on.

BEN. Admit it. Admit it. We got you. You weren't expecting it.

PAUL. Happy Birthday . . . (*Sets down cake.*)

BEN. O.K. Make a wish and blow out the candles.

SUSAN. (*Thinks.*) Got it. (*Blows out candles.*)

BEN. GERONIMO!!!!

SUSAN. Shhh, Ben the neighbors.

BEN. Well invite 'em over goddamn it. (*Yells down.*) WE'RE HAVING A PARTY!!!

SUSAN. I'll get the plates. Everybody want? (*Yes. Goes in.*)

BEN. And the champagne. Leave us never forget la champagne. (*Goes in.*)

PHIL. Your brother's a real character.

PAUL. Oh yeah. He's a real character all right. Actually, what he really is is he's a helluva guy.

PHIL. He told me this great joke. I don't know if you know it. Why aren't there any ice cubes in Poland? Do you know that one?

PAUL. There aren't any ice cubes in Poland? I'm sure that's not true.

PHIL. No. No, it's a joke.

PAUL. I was in Warsaw last year and we had cocktails at this hotel and I'm sure they had ice cubes. Yes, yes, they definitely did. I remember . . . ice cubes.

PHIL. No, you're supposed to . . .

JANICE. He's putting you on, honey. (PAUL *acknowledges this with good humor.*)

PHIL. (*Laughs quietly.*) You already heard it.

PAUL. He's my brother. We talk about everything. I'll tell you the problem I have with that joke, though.

I'm supposed to say 'why' and you're supposed to say 'the lady with the recipe died.' O.K., but the thing is, Poland's been trading a lot with the West, so even if this lady had forgotten to write the recipe down, let's say, and then let's say she died. Well, there's all these other people in Poland who would've come into contact with Europeans who had the recipe. So the whole premise of the joke is too far fetched to be genuinely amusing.

PHIL. You guys are both crazy.

PAUL. Why are we both crazy?

PHIL. What?

PAUL. Oh, I thought that was the beginning of another joke. Hey, I'm just feeling good.

PHIL. (*Laughs.*) Have you thought about that story idea at all?

PAUL. I have. I have thought about it.

PHIL. Do you think it could work? Tell me the truth.

PAUL. I think it could be very commercial.

PHIL. Seriously?

PAUL. Why not?

JANICE. Honey, what have you been bothering Paul about?

PHIL. I haven't been bothering him. I just asked him.

JANICE. Phil, nobody's going to want to make a movie about city planners. You think it's interesting because that's what you do. I told you not to bring it up . . .

PAUL. Now wait a minute. Wait a minute. I don't agree. I think if you handled it right there could be a big market for something like that. I'm telling you, people are sick and tired of violence and sex and glamour and fantasy. They want to see real life up on the screen.

PHIL. If I could write I'd do it myself, but I'm not really an artistic kind of person. I have it all up here. Like before I was just thinking about this one time when the computer broke down over at dispatch and all the busses got routed downtown to the city center. It was crazy. They were all lined up there bumper to bumper. People were yelling at each other. You should've seen it.

PAUL. Now that's what I'm saying. That's exactly the kind of thing that's missing from movies nowdays, scene like that. Busses all tangled up in the middle of town. (PAUL *hugs* PHIL. *Enter* SUSAN *with plates, followed by* BEN *with champagne.*)

BEN. . . . but I already made reservations. It's all set.

SUSAN. Well, you'll have to ask them about it. They're the ones that have to catch a flight.

BEN. Janice and Phil, may I have your undivided attention for just one moment? A suggestion has been made by yours truly that we celebrate Susan's birthday with a disgustingly lavish dinner tonight at the Four Seasons compliment of. Now, Susan has very reasonably pointed out that you two have to leave tonight, but I say nuts to that and furthermore, a certain company I work for happens to maintain a lovely suite of rooms at a very lovely hotel where you can stay after dinner and . . . And said company will provide you with a limousine to the airport tomorrow to meet any flight of your choosing. Now what do you say to that?

JANICE. Great!

BEN. Phil? Now think carefully before you say yes.

PHIL. Well, I'd really like to but . . .

JANICE. Honey, you don't have to be back at work on Monday . . .

PHIL. I was just thinking we shouldn't leave Jesse

with my folks for another day. We've already taken advantage of them.

JANICE. Sweetie, they love taking care of her. They'll spoil her rotten.

PHIL. Well, I guess we could call.

JANICE. We'll stay.

PHIL. Never argue with a lady.

BEN. I'll drink to that. O.K. Now I suggest we open the champagne, cut the cake and embarrass the hell out of Susan by watching her open all her presents. All in favor say nothing. Motion passed.

PAUL. Ben, you're really great, you know that.

BEN. Aw shucks, guy . . .

PAUL. No, really. I mean how many people would come all the way from England for a birthday? And this is the man who's broken every sales record in the history of Randle and Lane Securities, And, not only that, he's also managed to set up permanent offices in Spain, Greece, Italy, in East Germany. Where else, Ben? Have I missed any? Haven't you managed to break into a few other countries?

BEN. Let's get the presents.

JANICE. Phil, come on.

(BEN *exits into apartment.* PHIL *and* JANICE *follow.* PAUL *starts out.*)

SUSAN. Paul . . .

PAUL. Huh?

SUSAN. Don't do that to Ben. He means well.

PAUL. I have to get the present.

SUSAN. Paul.

PAUL. What?

SUSAN. What's going on?

PAUL. Nothing. (*Exits. Jet passes over.* SUSAN *watches.*)

BEN. (*Enters with two presents. Gives one to* SUSAN.) For you, my dear. Happy birthday.

SUSAN. What's that one?

BEN. Oh, just a little even-Steven, old family custom. Didn't Paul ever tell you about this? We always used to get a little even-Steven when the other one had a birthday. Dad had a theory it would prevent sibling rivalry. So much for *that* theory.

SUSAN. I'm sorry about the way he's behaving. I don't know what's going on. I really don't.

BEN. I'm used to it. (*Pause.*) It's a watch.

SUSAN. Good thinking.

(*Re-enter* PAUL *with* PHIL *and* JANICE, *bearing gifts.*)

BEN. Ah, here it comes. O.K., guy, hand it over and face the music.

PAUL. Me?

BEN. You know what they say about presents—lovers first. Theirs are always the worst. Friends later. Theirs are always greater.

PAUL. Do they say that? I didn't know. Happy birthday. (*Gives* SUSAN *present.*)

SUSAN. (*Surprised by coolness.*) Thank you. (*Starts to open it.*)

PAUL. I should explain this, by the way. I thought I'd get something really special this year and . . . there's these places midtown you never hear about. At least, I never did. They're shops, right, stores, like they sell things, but. Like where I found this thing. All they sell there is ancient Chinese treasures and you have to make an appointment to even get in the place. So . . . you're like the only customer. It's incredible. You get inside and you're in a different world. It's completely quiet. You can't hear any sounds from the street and all the stuff is under glass cases like a museum and the lady that shows you around says things like "Now here's an unusual little figurine . . . very rare T'ang Dynasty, perhaps you'd like me to take it out for you." I mean, that's what I call shopping. Do you like it? (SUSAN *holds up figurine of a horse. It has an opening in its back.*)

SUSAN. It's beautiful.

PAUL. Isn't it nice? Genuine Ming Dynasty. There's only about twenty of them in the world. That's what the lady said. They were only for the royal family. That's why I thought it was a nice idea. What they'd do is if the Emperor had a son that died before he was old enough to rule they'd cremate the body and put the ashes in that hole in the back and then they'd bury the whole works. I guess that's why they're so rare. But listen to this. This is the great part. It's shaped like a horse because they had this belief that the horse would take the child's spirit on a ride where it'd see its whole life passing by . . . the life it would have had if it hadn't died. And that way it could go to its final resting place in peace. At least that's what the lady explained.

BEN. Jesus, guy, this must've set you back a few pennies.

PAUL. Oh, yeah. But like I said, I wanted to get something really special and I think I got a pretty good deal. They were asking ninety-seven thousand, but I got 'em down to ninety-three. Not bad.

BEN. A steal at twice the price. (*They're getting uneasy.*)

PAUL. Still, I had to sell the business, all the editing machines, the office equipment, the lease on the building and I had to cash in my stocks and take out all my savings, but I finally scraped it all together.

SUSAN. Paul . . . ?

PAUL. I just thought it was worth it. We need something in this apartment for all the ashes. The unborn embryos. Isn't that what they do after they take 'em out. Don't they burn 'em, or did you have one of those guys that just pops it in a baggie and into the trash can . . . ?

SUSAN. Would you leave us alone, please.

BEN. Hey, guy, what is this . . .

SUSAN. Just leave us alone. All of you. Please. (BEN, PHIL *and* JANICE *exit inside.*)

PAUL. You mean you don't like it after all that?

SUSAN. Paul, is this for real?

PAUL. Is what for real?

SUSAN. This. (*The horse.*)

PAUL. Oh, yes. *That's* for real. . . . I thought you meant the embryo and I was going to ask you about that because it seems to have slipped your mind.

SUSAN. Is that what this is all about?

PAUL. I just thought it might be worth bringing up.

SUSAN. Who told you? Selina?

PAUL. Oh, is that what's important? Who told me? It wasn't you, that's for sure. And it's a pretty god damn weird thing to find out about from someone else. That you wife had an abortion six months ago and didn't bother to tell you about it. I guess I must just be one of those naturally curious people because when I found out it made me want to know all kinds of things, Susan. Like just what the fuck has been going on in our life? All these wonderful little human dramas going on under my nose and I didn't know a thing about it. Was it mine?

SUSAN. Yes.

PAUL. Why didn't you tell me?

SUSAN. Paul, I don't know. I really don't know. I meant to. I wanted to.

PAUL. I see. Anything else, or is that sort of the full explanation?

SUSAN. I don't know anything else. I didn't mean not to tell you.

PAUL. That's very illuminating. That really makes me feel like this is something we can work out. I mean what are we, Susan? Remind me because it's getting kind of vague in my mind. Are we married? Something like that? Is there some kind of unique relationship here? Something that might be worth looking into? Are you saying you didn't tell me because it isn't an interesting fact, or it's just not a very important thing for me to know about? Or it's an unpleasant topic of conversation or it's none of my business? I mean, what is this shit???

SUSAN. Stop it . . .

PAUL. SUSAN!!!!

BEN. (*Appears on terrace.*) Hey, is everything . . .

PAUL. GET OUT!!!

BEN. I'm just inside if . . .

PAUL. GET THE FUCK OUT OF HERE!!!! (BEN *retreats. Quiet.*) It hurts, Susan. It just hurts. All this silence between us. All this unknown stuff. You know how much I want a kid. You know that. I mean what've I been doing for the past three years? Running my ass off building up a business—working twelve hours a day? Am I supposed to have been doing that for the deep satisfaction it gave me? Do you think I'm a mental defective or something? I mean at very worst, I thought this was all some kind of weird test I was going through—some bizarre nest-building ritual to prove I was worthy of fertilizing your eggs. That was the only way I could look at it and still feel marginally sane . . .

SUSAN. I don't believe this. Are you saying you did everything you did so I'd let you make a baby? Is that what you're saying? Because if it is . . . well,

nice to know what you're keeping me around for.
Thank you.

PAUL. Susan, you know that's not what I meant.

SUSAN. All I know is it's a pretty shitty thing to lay
on me. Nobody forced you to do anything you didn't
want to do. So what's this thing like it's all been some
kind of terrible ordeal? Jesus, Paul, what's the matter
with you? You are allowed to enjoy it, you know.
There's no law that says you have to feel terrible
about it. You earned it, for god sake. You deserve it.
And I'm proud of you, babe. I really am. I just want
to see you be happy with it.

PAUL. Ah, so that's why you had the abortion.
That's why you didn't tell me—because you wanted
me to be happy. You were doing it all for me. Gee,
why didn't I see it that way? We really are wonderful
people, aren't we Susan? We just do everything for
each other.

SUSAN. All right. I didn't tell you. I was wrong—
mea culpa. What can I say, Paul? I'm sorry? Because
I am. But that doesn't have very much to do with
anything right now, does it?

PAUL. But why? Why?

SUSAN. Babe, you don't get a whole lot of time to
think about what you should do when there's this thing
growing inside you. And it's not getting smaller. And
the more you think things over the less small it's getting. It's not like I just popped down to the friendly
neighborhood abortionist. I did think it over just a
little bit before I went through with it.

PAUL. But why didn't you say anything?

SUSAN. (*Quiet.*) Paul. I like what we have. I guess
I just don't want anything to change it all.

PAUL. And telling me would have changed it all.

SUSAN. I don't know. Wouldn't it?

PAUL. Well, if it would then what the hell is it we have that's so great?

SUSAN. Oh, so now we have nothing . . .

PAUL. Well tell me, Susan, what do we have? Tell me what we have . . .

SUSAN. Everything you've done. Everything I've done. Everything we've got. It's all nothing? None of it means anything to you? My god, Paul, how you must be suffering.

PAUL. We really hate each other, don't we?

SUSAN. Babe, I don't hate you. I just don't understand why we always make everything so complicated for each other. Hasn't this been a good time? I mean, I was under the impression we were more or less happy. In fact, I was even thinking if Greg and Francine get divorced we'll be the longest couple of all our friends.

PAUL. Except for Doug and Maraya.

SUSAN. That doesn't count. They're not married. Shit!

PAUL. What?

SUSAN. I'm smoking. (*They smile.*)

PAUL. I don't know what it is, Susan. I mean, yes, I want all this. Sometimes. Sometimes I'm really amazed it's me that's doing all this. There's been whole weeks when I went around thinking, "hey, this is a pretty good deal. I'm happy." I mean, this is it, right? This must be it. I must be happy. But then one day I'll come home, I'll go in there and try to get comfortable, read or something and for some reason I just can't concentrate. Try to watch TV, can't even manage that. So I start walking around the apartment and I see all the stuff we have. All this stuff. And I start thinking about what we do to get it. You pick up a little box and go click. I tape together pieces of film. Presto. We have everything we want. We're so good at doing these little things that make us able to have all this stuff, but we can't get it together to have one stupid little baby. Us. The two of us. Together. Doesn't that ever seem strange to you? You know, sort of intuitively wrong? Absurd. Something like that?

SUSAN. No, Paul. I'm sorry, it doesn't. The only thing I find strange is the way I keep feeling like I have to have a baby to be enough for you. I mean, what if I decide a baby isn't as important to me as a lot of other things? What happens if I decide that all I want is you? And our life together? And our work? I mean, couldn't that be enough? Paul. (*Pause.*) Paul. Paul, answer me. Am I enough for you without a baby? (*Pause.*) I see. And you wanted to know why I couldn't tell you. ◂

PAUL. I don't know. I don't know. Why didn't you say something before this?

SUSAN. Maybe I didn't want to know what I just found out. Well, Paul, I'm sorry. I'm sorry you feel so badly about your accomplishments because I'm feeling pretty good about mine and I can't see any reason why I shouldn't. Doug starts doing well, you laugh about it. You think it's funny. You do well and suddenly it's wrong. I don't get it. You can't have it all ways, babe. We're not children any more. You have what you have. If you want it, keep it and stop making excuses for it. And if you want to be a saint, go back and dig outhouses for the Nglele.

PAUL. Oh boy.

SUSAN. What?

PAUL. We're in a lot of trouble, aren't we?

SUSAN. I guess we are.

PAUL. So now what?

SUSAN. I don't know. Should we be talking about this now?

PAUL. No. I want to go out and have a great time
with Ben and Janice and Phil.

SUSAN. All right. We'll talk about it now. What are
we going to do?

PAUL. I don't know.

SUSAN. Well, we're going to have to do something,
aren't we?

PAUL. Like a divorce, you mean?

SUSAN. Is that what you want?

PAUL. Do you?

SUSAN. Well, I hadn't exactly been thinking about
it a whole lot. Not today. Are you serious?

PAUL. Isn't that what's going on here? Can you
think of anything else we could do?

SUSAN. Well, well, happy birthday.

PAUL. I meant it to hurt, Susan.

SUSAN. Yes. We'll call a lawyer in the morning.

PAUL. Lawyer? (*Pause.*) O.K.

SUSAN. Fine.

PAUL. Jesus. (*Plane flies over. They look at each
other. Blackout.*)

SCENE 8

*Slide: 1979. The cabin, winter, snow outside. Early
evening. Open pot-belly stove with fire. Old
couch with crochet-square afghan covering it.*
PAUL *and* SUSAN *wrapped in blankets, naked beneath.* PAUL *sits on couch.* SUSAN *showing slides
on wall from projector with a carousel. Slide of*
DOUG *and* MARAYA *and three children standing
proudly in front of construction firm's office building. Then the carousel is at an end leaving white
square on wall.*

PAUL. Wait a minute. Go back. Let me see the last

one again. (SUSAN *backs up to* DOUG *and* MARAYA *and family.*) Doug and Maraya. He shaved off his beard.

SUSAN. Yeah, a couple of months ago. That's his office. I used it for background on a job. (*Turns the lights on.*) I think he's a little upset you haven't been in touch.

PAUL. It's the first time I've been back east.

SUSAN. You could've called. Written a letter.

PAUL. Hey.

SUSAN. What?

PAUL. This is real nice. I'd sort of forgotten. Well, I hadn't forgotten, but I hadn't remembered with total accuracy if you know what I mean.

SUSAN. I think I know what you mean.

PAUL. So you actually went and bought this place.

SUSAN. Yeah, nostalgia. I got a good deal. The Pearsons let me have it cheap because we'd been married here. They're sentimental.

PAUL. Opportunist.

SUSAN. How come you haven't been in touch with anyone? Selina was asking about you. Gary and Linda. Even Lawrence. You hiding in San Francisco?

PAUL. No, I just . . . it didn't feel real until the divorce came through. I don't know. I just didn't want to think about all that.

SUSAN. Who's Edie?

PAUL. Edie? (SUSAN *exits into bedroom, keeps talking.*)

SUSAN. (*Off.*) Yeah. I called you in San Francisco a couple months ago and someone called Edie answered the phone.

PAUL. Oh. She never said anything.

SUSAN. (*Off.*) What?

PAUL. I said she never said anything.

SUSAN. (*Off.*) I didn't tell her who I was.

PAUL. More secrets, huh.

SUSAN. (*Off.*) Who is she?

PAUL. Just a woman I'm seeing.

SUSAN. (*Off.*) Ah-hah. Seeing a woman called Edie, eh?

PAUL. She's nice. She has a kid.

SUSAN. (*Off.*) Is it serious?

PAUL. I don't know. She's a photographer, speaking of making the same mistake twice. (SUSAN *enters, dressing.* PAUL *puts wood in the stove.*)

SUSAN. You're kidding.

PAUL. Not only that. She picked the same yellow tiles for her bathroom as you picked for ours.

SUSAN. She has good taste.

PAUL. Well, she picked me.

SUSAN. Are you happy?

PAUL. Happy? Why? I mean, yeah. I guess so. What about you?

SUSAN. Oh, I'm O.K. It's just . . . like this. Today, being with you again, I just started remembering how nice it was. Sometimes. When it was nice. We should've married other people and had a long affair.

PAUL. It's a nice school where I'm teaching. Nice kids. Very bright. Rich, of course. I like it, though. I really do. I guess I'm happy.

SUSAN. Good.

PAUL. Hey.

SUSAN. Do you do that with Edie? Say "hey?"

PAUL. Come here.

SUSAN. (*Watching him.*) I knew it'd happen like this. You'd just show up all of a sudden. Wouldn't phone. I'd've been able to say no if you phoned. It's funny how we can't seem to keep our hands off each other, even now.

PAUL. Come here.

SUSAN. Hang on a second. (*Exits again. Off.*) How's Ben doing?

PAUL. Better. They did a cardiogram and discovered he'd had another heart attack three years before this one. Hadn't even known about it. Just cured himself.

SUSAN. (*Off.*) Still drinking?

PAUL. Not for now. What are you doing in there?

SUSAN. (*Off.*) Looking for my boots.

PAUL. What are you getting dressed for? Let's raid the ice-box. It's almost time for . . . (*Watch.*) jesus, it's only five. I forgot how early it gets dark up here in the winter.

SUSAN. (*Off.*) Go ahead. Help yourself. I think there's some chicken.

PAUL. Aren't you hungry? You always used to get hungry afterwards.

SUSAN. (*Enters, dressed.*) How do I look?

PAUL. Terrible. Come here.

SUSAN. Why don't you get some food?

PAUL. Are you going somewhere?

SUSAN. Paul, I have a life. I can't just stop everything just because you show up unannounced. I'd made plans for dinner.

PAUL. Oh, you didn't say.

SUSAN. I wasn't really expecting anything like this to happen. It didn't leave much time for talking, did it.

PAUL. No, I guess not. Who's the lucky man?

SUSAN. You don't know him.

PAUL. What's his name?

SUSAN. Jerry.

PAUL. He's coming here?

SUSAN. Don't worry. I'll go out to the car.

PAUL. Can I come? Sorry. Can I wait for you?

SUSAN. I don't think that'd be a very good idea.

PAUL. You're coming back with him?

SUSAN. We usually do.

PAUL. You see him a lot, huh?

SUSAN. He has a place near here. It's convenient.
He lives in New York. He's an illustrator, He's 5'11",
165 pounds, vegetarian, blue eyes. Anything else you'd
like to know?

PAUL. He sounds fabulous.

SUSAN. He's all right. Actually, he's very nice.

PAUL. Nice. Funny, that's what I said about Edie.
Maybe we should introduce them. When'll I see you
again?

SUSAN. When'll you be back east?

PAUL. Depends. I might come back real soon if you
made me a good offer. Another dirty weekend in New
Hampshire.

SUSAN. I don't think we should do this again.

PAUL. Why not?

SUSAN. Well . . . we're being unfaithful. I don't
know, Paul. I guess you just don't get over nine years
so easily. I don't.

PAUL. No. (*Car noise outside.*)

SUSAN. Jesus, he's early. What time is it? (PAUL
has a watch.)

PAUL. Ten past.

SUSAN. Damn. Do I look O.K.? Sorry. Listen, when
you go just throw a few logs on the fire and make sure
the damper's turned down. Bye, Paul. (SUSAN *takes
winter coat and starts out door. Stops. Yells outside . . .*) HANG ON, JERRY, I'LL BE RIGHT
OUT. I . . . I FORGOT MY BAG. (SUSAN *comes
back into room. She and* PAUL *embrace, kiss, hold each
other. Then it's over.*) Bye, babe.

PAUL. Bye. (SUSAN *goes.* PAUL *watches car from
window. When it's gone he sits, turns on projector,
watches slides. Fade.*)

PROPERTY LIST

— pre-set
 * Character carries on during course of show
   Brace—carried on all at once by character

SCENE 1:

— pink t-shirt of PAUL's
— remnants of beach fire (sticks of wood, glued together)
  Center Right Stage (hole to put out cigarettes)
— cigarette pack of PAUL's (Center Right Stage)
— Bic lighter of PAUL's (Center Right Stage)
 * carpet shoulder bag—JANICE
 * fake money—in carpet shoulder bag—JANICE
 * flashlight (small)—JANICE (extra batteries)
 * fish (fresh and large)—BALINESE FISHERMAN

SCENE 2:

— tree with clothesline (diapers, towels, etc.—Upstage Right
— tree stump (Center Right Stage)
— wood frame (4' x 6'—Center Left Stage)
— saw horse (Downstage Left)
— 2' x 4' board (leaning against saw horse)
— blue hand towel (Upstage Left of frame)

COSTUME

— PAUL's shirt (yellow plaid—Downstage Right)

COSTUME

— DOUG's shirt (plaid—Upstage of tree stump)
— Cigarette Pack (in PAUL's shirt)
— Bic lighter (in PAUL's shirt)
 * 2' x 4' board—pre-cut in two pieces ⎫
 * hand-saw   ⎬ PAUL
 * piece of bread with mayonnaise ⎫
 * knife   ⎪
 * diaper   ⎬ MARAYA
 * clothes-pin   ⎪
 * camera ⎫
 * ½ apple ⎬ SUSAN
 * canvas picnic folding chair (Blue) ⎫
 * two beer cans (one empty, one filled with water) ⎬ DOUG
 * plate with sandwiches   ⎫
 * three closed Coke cans with plastic holder   ⎪
 * quilted blanket   ⎬ MARAYA
 * BABY JAKE   ⎪

87

COSTUME
— two glycerine for sweat (PAUL and DOUG)

SCENE 3:
— round iron table (white—Off Center Left)
— three folding chairs (white—one Down of table, one Up of
    table, one Right of table)
— swing set (check chains and bolts—Downstage Right)
— picket gate fence (white and aged—Upstage Left)
— On Iron Table:
    — bottle of rubber cement
    — rag
    — two large panels with photographs
      (one with empty spaces—Down Chair pre-set on Iron
      table)
— On Up Chair:
    — wooden Coke carton
    — two small photos (for gluing) in Coke carton   ⎫
    * portable radio (on Right Chair—Stop/Play/   ⎬ SUSAN
      Stop: classical music)   ⎭

COSTUME
* blue jean apron (SUSAN)
* paper shopping bag   ⎫
* In Shopping Bag: ⎬ BEN
    * two plastic glasses
    * bottle of Dom Perignon Champagne
      (Filled with 7UP and able to pop cork)   ⎭

SCENE 4:
— daybed with cover (Upstage Center)
— weaved rug (square-striped—Center Stage)
— four pillows (three floor [India print]—Downstage Left;
    one On daybed—Upstage Center)
— green armchair with throw (aged—Downstage Right)
— wooden end table (Right of Armchair)
— On End Table:
    —script with felt marker pen (opened)
    — pencils (sharp)
    — ashtray with butts
    — cigarette pack (PAUL's)
    — Bic lighter (PAUL's)
    — magazines and scripts underneath
— large wooden table (Right of daybed)
— On top of Table:
    — glass with pens and pencils (sharp)
    — beer can (empty)

— black script
— yellow legal pad (On Black Script)
— black telephone
— cigarette pack (SELINA's)
— Bic lighter (SELINA's)
COSTUME
— suede shoulder bag (JANICE's)
 * beer can (filled with water)—PAUL
 * plate with four Hostess cupcakes—PAUL
 * two coffee mugs—SELINA
COSTUME
 * pink straw traveling bag }
 * carpet shoulder bag   } SUSAN
SCENE 5:
— two park benches (Off Center Left—Off Center Right)
— large park wastecan (filled with debris—Down of Left
    bench)
— plastic toy frog (Underneath Left Bench)
— Kentucky Fried Chicken basket (filled with debris—Center
    of Right bench)
— dirty napkin (next to basket—Center of Right bench)
— two beer cans (one empty on ground of corner Right
    bench; half-filled with water for PAUL; up corner Left
    bench)
— two toys (one ball, one truck)—underneath Center of
    Right bench
COSTUME
— DOUG's jacket (Up corner of Right bench)
COSTUME
— SUSAN's canvas shoulder bag (Up corner of Left bench)
COSTUME
— cigarettes and lighter in SUSAN's shoulder bag
 * BABY MATTIE—PAUL
 * Kentucky Fried Chicken, Coke cup (with cover and straw)
    —SUSAN
 * blue cloth carry shoulder bag   )
 * In Shoulder Bag:)
    * baby bottle in holder   )
    * bib   ) MARAYA
    * towel   )
    * baby cap   )
    * small blanket   )
SCENE 6:
— two large paint tarps (sewn together)

— modern standing lamp (silver chrome—Upstage Right)
— Director's chair (biege canvas—under head of lamp)
— painter's ladder (aged—Downstage Left)
— On Ladder Rung (pasted together):
    — roller set (tray and roller)
    —sponge
    — rag
— two of SUSAN's framed photos leaning against Right of
    ladder on floor (one row of spoons; two plates of fruit)
— On Floor (Center Stage Left):
    —four cans of paint (two large, two small and new)
    — can of paint remover
    — plastic glove (with paint on it)
    — paint brush
— waste can (white—Upstage of paint cans)
— black script binder (top of Director's chair)
— biege telephone (on floor—Center of Left side of carton)
— cardboard carton (two holes for carrying)
— silver serving tray (aluminum—top of cardboard carton)
— On Silver Serving Tray:
    — Chinese take-out carton
    — chop-sticks (in take-out carton)
    — bottle of wine (cheap, filled with water)
    — cigarettes
    — lighter
    — ashtray with butts
    — fortune cookie
 * Chinese take-out carton   ⎫
 * chop-sticks (In take-out carton) ⎬ SUSAN
 * fortune cookie   ⎭

COSTUME
 * brown leather traveling bag ⎫
 * airline ticket   ⎪
 * In PAUL's Coat pocket: ⎬ PAUL
   * Joint holder ⎪
   * cigarette   ⎪
   * lighter   ⎭

SCENE 6:
 * Canvas and leather shoulder bag with liner ⎫
 * In Shoulder Bag: ⎪
 * two bottles of cheap champagne (one ⎬ LAWRENCE
    filled with 7UP and able to pop cork) ⎪
 * T.V. Guide ⎭

SCENE 7:
— four corner terrace walls/balcony:
   (two with long ends (1) Upstage Left (2) Upstage Right);
   (two with short ends (1) Downstage Left (2) Downstage
   Right)
— terrace wooden table (white—up of Downstage Left wall)
— two wooden matching chairs to table (brown and white
   covers—(1) up of table; (2) Down of table
— two chaise lounges with covers (brown and white)—(1)
   Upstage Left; (2) Upstage Right
— barbeque (able to open—in corner of Right wall)
— wooden coffee table (two pieces, white, matching); (furni-
   ture between chaises)
— On Wooden Coffee Table:
   — two rock glasses (filled with water and lemon peel)
   — lighter
   — glass holder for cigarettes
   — cigarettes in glass holder
   — matches
   — ashtray (glass, glued to table)
COSTUME
— cigarette purse (JANICE's)
 * birthday cake with candles } PAUL
 * cake plate
 * silver serving tray
 * On Silver Serving Tray:
   * five champagne glasses
   * cake knife
   * five forks (silver) } BEN
   * bottle of Dom Perignon Champagne (filled
     with 7UP and able to pop cork)
 * five cake dishes—SUSAN
 * six birthday presents (gifts-wrapped)
 * In Wooden Box with Velvet Lining
   * horse (Ming Dynasty—Jade, with hole in back) } PAUL
 * two small boxes—(1) watch for PAUL; (2) for SUSAN—BEN
 * large box from—PHIL
 * two small boxes from—JANICE
SCENE 8:
— couch (wicker—Upstage Center)
— On Wicker Couch:
   — quilted throw
   — velvet pillow

— standing lamp with shade (Old-fashioned, working lamp; Up of Right corner of couch)
— weaved rug (Round, 6'—in front of couch)
— wicker arm chair with pillow seat (Down Left of Rug)
— small wooden end table (Left of couch)
— carousel projector (working—on top of end table)
— stove (able to open top—Upstage Right)
— wood pile with holder (Right of stove—on floor)
— rag (under small piece of wood for PAUL's use)
— small piece of cut wood (in pile for PAUL's use)
— couch (wicker—Upstage Center)
— On Wicker Couch:
COSTUME
— blue jeans of PAUL's (pre-set on couch)
COSTUME
— shirt of PAUL's (pre-set on couch)
COSTUME
— watch of PAUL's (pre-set underneath table)
COSTUME
* two blankets (1) blue, electric—SUSAN; (2) brown—PAUL
COSTUME
* tan knee socks—SUSAN
COSTUME
* brown leather shoulder bag
* In Shoulder Bag: }
    * brush
    * blusher and lipstick   } SUSAN
    * perfume

COSTUME PLOT

PAUL:
SCENE 1:
Army fatigue pants (legts rolled up)
pink t-shirt (faded)
bathing suit (blue)
bare feet
costume and prop (t-shirt—pre-set); (cigarette pack and Bic
    lighter—pre-set)
SCENE 2:
blue jeans
work boots
hiking socks
plaid shirt (yellow)
costume and prop (shirt—pre-set)
SCENE 3
wedding ring—on
corduroy pants (tan)
leather belt
blue work shirt (aged—snaps)
sneakers (aged)
socks
wedding ring
SCENE 4:
khaki pants (green)
grey sweat shirt
blue cord shirt
socks
stocking feet
SCENE 5:
dress blue jeans
belt
matching jean jacket
grey striped shirt
tie-shoes (brown—casual)
socks
SCENE 6:
white suit
blue striped shirt
tie (funky large print)

white perforated shoes
white socks
sunglasses
costume and prop (airline ticket) right pocket of jacket;
    (joints in holder) right pocket of jacket; (cigarettes and
    lighter) left pocket of jacket
SCENE 7:
biege line slacks
blue Adolpho shirt
light brown perforated shoes
socks
SCENE 8:
wedding ring (off)
brown blanket
bare feet
costume and prop (watch—pre-set; pants and shirt—pre-set
    on couch)

SUSAN:
SCENE 1:
lavender leotard bathing suit
blue jeans (patched and faded)
barefoot
SCENE 2:
over-alls (faded)
Indian shirt (orange trim)
corky sandals
socks (red-striped)
prop (camera)
SCENE 3:
wedding ring—on
India sundress
Dr. Scholl sandals
costume and prop (blue jean apron; wedding ring; eyeglasses)
SCENE 4:
Ukranian blouse
blue jean skirt (flare)
black high-heel boots
red belt—woven
necklace
stockings and slip
costume and prop (pink design straw traveling bag; shoulder-
    bag—carpet)

SCENE 5:
khaki pants (biege)   } matching
safari-jacket (biege) }
blue shirt
belt (blue-striped)
tassel loafers (brown)
stockings
watch
costume and prop (shoulder-bag [canvas]—pre-set; cigarette
    and Bic lighter in shoulder bag)
SCENE 6:
green linen slacks
yellow blouse (tunic)
grasshopper mules (off-white)
stockings
gold earrings
watch
SCENE 7:
yellow silk dress
sling-back shoes (beige)
stocking and slip
sunglasses
SCENE 8:
wedding ring—off
blue electric blanket
pink panties and bra
tan knee socks
rust blouse
tan fitted slacks
brown belt
brown boots
costume and prop (fur coat or coat—pre-set; chain necklace;
    brown leather shoulder-bag
costume and prop (in bag)—brush; blusher and lipstick;
    perfume

SELINA: ·
SCENE 3:
print skirt (red design—flare)
peach t-shirt
corky sandals
slip
earrings
sunglasses

costume and prop (straw handbag)
SCENE 4:
red blouse
blue jeans
sandals
earrings
SCENE 6:
red jeans
beige sweater (round collar)
thongs
turquoise Indian necklace
earrings

JANICE:
SCENE 1:
appliqued jeans (patched and faded)
mirrored blue India blouse
beaded necklace
costume and prop (shoulder carpet bag; money in bag)
SCENE 4:
long beige India tunic
beige India draw-string pants
head band
Marachi sandals
necklace
costume and prop (suede-fringed shoulder bag—pre-set)
SCENE 7:
wedding ring—on
pink silk tunic blouse
white wool pleated slacks
beige high-heel sandals
stockings
costume jewelry (a lot of)
wedding ring
prop (cigarette purse and Bic lighter—pre-set)

MARAYA:
SCENE 2:
print skirt (flowered)
beige India blouse
weaved sandals
SCENE 5:
maternity dress (blue-plaid)
brown espadrills

maternity pad
stockings and slip
costume and prop (blue cloth carry shoulder bag)
costume and prop (in bag)—baby bottle—no holder; bib;
    towel; baby cap; small blanket

BEN:
SCENE 3:
beige seer-sucker suit (two-piece)
yellow shirt
tie (blue and brown—striped)
brown tie shoes (business)
brown leather belt
brown socks
wedding ring
SCENE 7:
tan blazer
beige slacks
brown striped shirt
brown leather belt
tie (design)
socks
wedding ring

DOUG:
SCENE 2:
Army fatigue pants (aged)
ski-boots
white socks
costume and prop (plaid shirt—pre-set; tool belt)
prop (in tool belt)—hammer; nails; tape measure; t-square
SCENE 5:
olive three-piece suit (casual—plaid lining)
white shirt
maroon tie
brown tie-shoes (casual)
brown socks
wrapped hand (right)

LAWRENCE:
SCENE 6:
blue blazer
yellow shirt
beige slacks

tan loafers
tan socks
sunglasses
gold necklace
costume and prop (leather and canvas shoulder-bag)
RUSSELL:
SCENE 4:
beige India tunic
beige India draw-string pants
sandals
bracelet
leather shoulder-pouch

PHIL:
SCENE 7:
blue whip-cord suit (two-piece—Brooks Brothers)
white shirt
blue tie
brown tie-shoes (business)
brown socks
wedding ring

BALINESE FISHERMAN:
SCENE 1:
t-shirt
sarong (print)
sandals
belt
hand band
under pants

BABY JAKE:
SCENE 2:
costume and prop (yellow baby blanket)

BABY MATTIE:
SCENE 5:
costume and prop (green blanket; yellow cap; blue jumper;
    blue sneakers

COSTUME PLOT

PAUL
2 blue Adolfo shirts
2 blue striped shirts
1 beige striped shirt
1 blue corduroy shirt
1 blue work shirt
2 pair jeans
1 jean jacket
1 pair olive work pants (rolled)
1 pair gold corduroy pants
1 pair linen pants
2 grey t-shirts
1 white suit
4 pair shoes:
   1 pair work boots
   1 pair work shoes
   1 pair white suede
   1 pair tan suede
1 pair Sneakers
accessories:
   1 tie
   3 pairs socks
   1 pair glasses
   1 cigarette case
   2 belts
1 pink t-shirt
1 pair green pants
1 Snuff box

JANICE
1 blue blouse
1 pair dungarees
1 Guru top and pants
1 pink blouse
1 pair white slacks
1 body suit
1 pair sandals
1 pair shoes

SELINA
1 red flowered skirt
2 peach shirts

1 pair dungarees
1 burgandy blouse
1 pair red slacks
1 tan sweater
1 pair sandals
1 pair thongs

SUSAN

1 bathing suit
1 pair dungarees
1 pair overalls
1 Indian blouse
1 sun dress
1 pair khaki pants
1 blue shirt
2 yellow dresses
1 set pink undies
1 pair tan slacks
shoes:
   1 pair slip-ons
   1 pair sandals
   1 pair walking shoes
   1 pair Dr. Scholl's
   1 pair black boots
   1 pair strap shoes
   1 pair low, brown boot-shoes
2 pair tan knee socks
2 pair underpants
1 half slip (white)
1 yellow blouse
1 pair blue slacks
2 belts

DOUG

2 white shirts
1 flannel, blue plaid shirt
1 pair dungarees
1 3-piece tan suit
1 belt
1 tie
1 pair boot-shoes
1 neck tie
1 white shirt

LAWRENCE

1 blue jacket
1 pair tan slacks

2 yellow shirts
1 pair light brown, slip-on shoes

BALINESE FISHERMAN

2 pair black tights
2 torn shirts
two-piece fabric shirt and belt
1 fabric headband
1 pair dungarees

MARAYA

1 peasant skirt and belt
1 peasant blouse
1 blue plaid dress and belt
1 half-slip
1 set padded undergarments
1 padded bra
1 pair sandals
1 pair brown shoes

BEN

1 pin-stripe suit
1 tan jacket
1 pair tan trousers
2 blue shirts
2 striped shirts
2 neck ties
1 pair brown, wing-tip shoes

BABY THINGS

3 blankets
1 sleeper
2 hats

RUSSELL

1 Guru suit
2 undershirts
1 pair sandals
1 accessory pocketbook
1 necklace

PHIL

1 pin-stripe suit
2 white shirts
1 pair brown shoes
1 tie
1 belt
1 pair glasses
1 tie clip

PROPERTIES

red faded t-shirt of Paul's
remnants of beach fire—sticks of wood, hole to put out ciga-
    rette, cigarette pack and matches
*cloth bag—JANICE—with money in it
*flashlight—JANICE
*fish (large)—FISHERMAN
SCENE 2
tree with clothesline (diapers, towels, etc.)
tree stump
wood frame—4' x 6'
saw horse
blue towel
PAUL's shirt—yellow plaid—cigarette and matches inside
DOUG's shirt
*2—2x4 piece of wood (from 1 large piece of 2x4 wood cut into
    2 by PAUL)
*handsaw—PAUL
*tool belt—hammer, nails, measuring tape—DOUG
*1 camera—SUSAN
*½ apple—SUSAN
*1 blue folding chair
*2 beer cans—1 empty, 1 full—DOUG
*piece of bread with mayo and knife—MARAYA
*diaper with clothespin—MARAYA
*plate of sandwiches—MARAYA
*2 closed Coke cans with plastic holder—MARAYA
*quilted blanket—MARAYA
*BABY JAKE—MARAYA
costume-prop—glycerine for sweat
SCENE 3
1 round table
2 folding chairs
1 swing set—check chain and bolts
gate
on table—rubber cement, rag, eyeglasses
2 large photograph panels—1 with empty spaces
1 loose photo

* Characters carries on during the course of the show.

wooden Coke carton
*portable radio—rewind-stop-play-stop—Susan
*1 blue jean apron—Susan
*1 paper shopping bag with/liner—Ben
in shopping bag—2 plastic glasses, 1 bottle of Dom Perignon
    champagne (must be able to pop-fill with 7up)

Scene 4

daybed with cover
strip rug
3 floor pillows—print
1 green armchair with throw
small wooden table
on table:
  script with felt marker pen (open script)
  sharp pencils
  ashtray with butts
  matches
  magazines or scripts underneath
large table
on table:
  glass with pens and sharp pencils
  empty beer can
  black script
  yellow legal pad on top of script
  black telephone
  costume-prop—suede bag of Janice's
  cigarettes and lighter
*beer can with H2O—Paul
*plate of cupcakes (4)—Paul
*2 coffee mugs—Selina
costume-prop—*pink straw traveling bag—Susan

Scene 5

2 park benches
large park waste can filled with garbage
toy frog (hidden under Left bench)
Kentucky Fried Chicken basket filled with bones, napkins, etc.
dirty napkin (Right Center bench, next to basket)
2 beer cans—1 empty (Right Center bench on the ground), 1
  ½ filled with H2O (Left bench upcorner)
2 toys—1 ball, 1 truck (both Right bench Center, underneath)
costume-prop:
  Doug's jacket—Right bench upcorner; Susan's shoulder bag—
    Left bench upcorner; matches and cigarettes in Paul's
    jean jacket pocket; Doug's hand bandage

*Baby Mattie—Paul
*Kentucky Fried Chicken Coke cup with cover and straw—
    Susan
*1 blue cloth carry-all pause—Maraya
inside purse—baby bottle in holder, bib, cloth, towel, etc.
Scene 6
2 large drop cloths (tarps) sewn together
modern standing lamp—silver chrome
director's chair—beige
painter's ladder
on paint can rung, pasted together—roller set (tray and roller);
    sponge; rag
2 of Susan's framed photos—(1) row of spoons leaning against
    each other, (2) plate of fruit on floor Left
4 scripts—film, old green, script, new green script Left of ladder
    on floor
pasted together:
    2 paint cans
    1 can of paint remover
    1 plastic glove with paint on it
    paint brush
white waste can—next to paint buckets, etc.
black script binder—top of seat of director's chair
beige telephone—Left Center of box carton
box carton with hole at top and bottom for carrying
silver serving tray-aluminium- on top of carton
On silver serving tray:
    3 paper cups
    2 Chinese take-out cartons with chop sticks—1 preset on tray
    *1 taken in by Susan at start of scene
    bottle of cheap wine filled ¾'s
    cigarettes and lighter
    glass ashtray with butts
    2 fortune cookies—1 preset on tray, *1 taken in by Susan
        at start of scene
carton at angle
costume-prop—*brown leather traveling bag—Paul
*man's shoulder bag with with liner—Lawrence
in bag:
    2 bottles of inexpensive champagne, 1 full and closed, 1 filled
        and able to pop open
costume-prop—(In Paul's coat pocket):
    *Airline ticket

*Joint holder
*cigarette lighter
*TV Guide—LAWRENCE
SCENE 7
4 corner terrace balcony pieces
2 matching terrace chairs
terrace table
2 chaises, 1 with ashtray glued to right arm
barbeque (able to open)
coffee table to match chairs, table and chaises
on top of coffee table:
  2 glasses filled with H2O and lemon slice
  lighter
  cigarette case—JANICE's
  cigarettes in glass holder
  matches
  ashtray (glued down)
*Birthday cake with candles on cake tray—PAUL
silver serving tray
on serving tray (*BEN):
  *5 champagne glasses
  *cake knife
  *forks (silver)
  *5 plates, 2 carried on by SUSAN
  bottle of champagne, able to pop—*BEN
*6 presents:
  1 Ming Dynasty horse with hole in back (jade), wrapped in
    box with velvet—PAUL
  2 small presents wrapped (1 for SUSAN, watch for PAUL)—
    BEN
  1 large box from—PHIL
  2 small, wrapped—JANICE
SCENE 8
1 old fashioned couch
present on couch:
  quilted patchwork throw
  velvet pillow
  PAUL's jeans (costume-prop)
  PAUL's sweater or shirt (costume-prop)
Working, old fashioned standing lamp with shade
6' round hooked rug
wicker arm chair
SUSAN's fur coat, costume-prop, on chair
small wooden end table

on table:
  carousel projector-works electrically
  PAUL'S watch (costume-prop) underneath table
stove
wood pile with holder
rag (under small piece of wood pile)
*2 blankets (costume-prop), *1 blue, electric—SUSAN; *1 brown,
    electric—PAUL
*shoulder bag of SUSAN'S (costume-prop), leather
inside bag: perfume, makeup, mirror
*SUSAN'S socks (costume-prop)

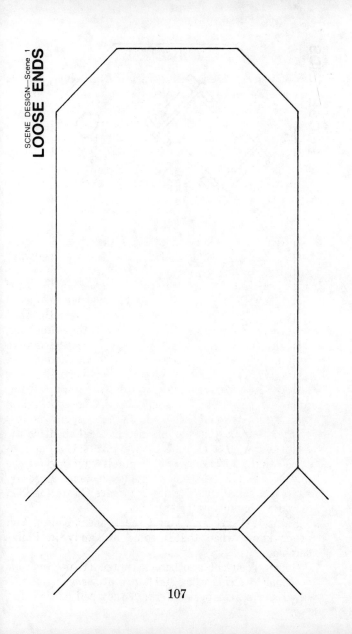

TREE STUMP

SAWHORSES &
WINDOW FRAMES

TREE STUMP

TO TRUCK

TO TRAILER

WASH-LINE

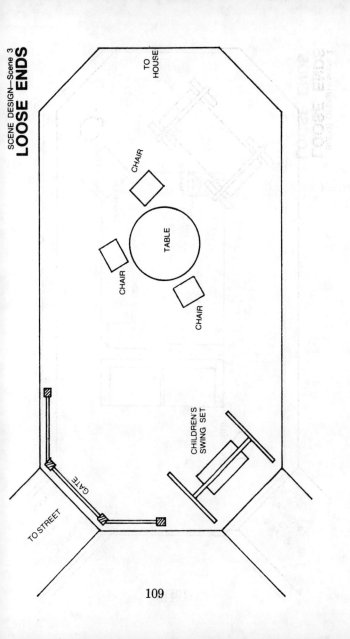

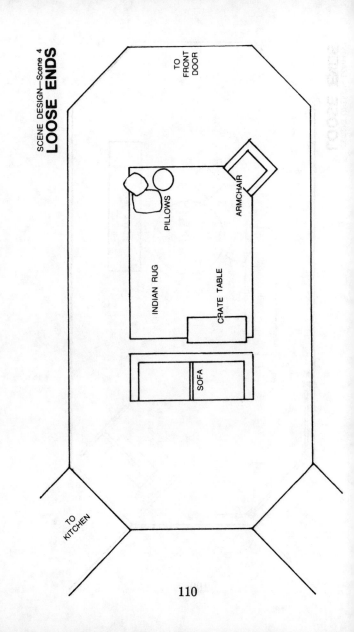

SCENE DESIGN—Scene 4
LOOSE ENDS

TO FRONT DOOR

PILLOWS

INDIAN RUG

ARMCHAIR

CRATE TABLE

SOFA

TO KITCHEN

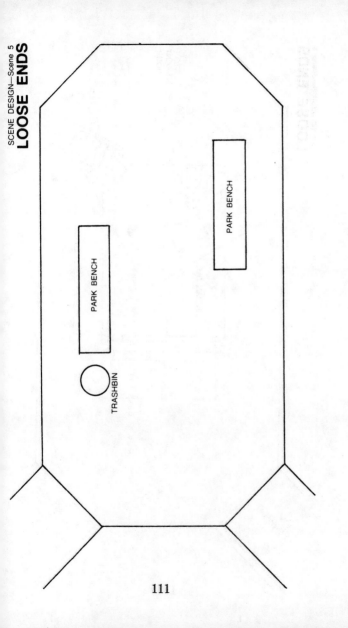

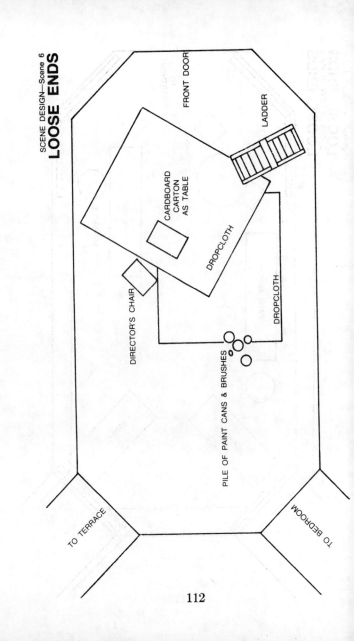

SCENE DESIGN—Scene 6
LOOSE ENDS

FRONT DOOR

LADDER

CARDBOARD
CARTON
AS TABLE

DROPCLOTH

DROPCLOTH

DIRECTOR'S CHAIR

PILE OF PAINT CANS & BRUSHES

TO TERRACE

TO BEDROOM

112

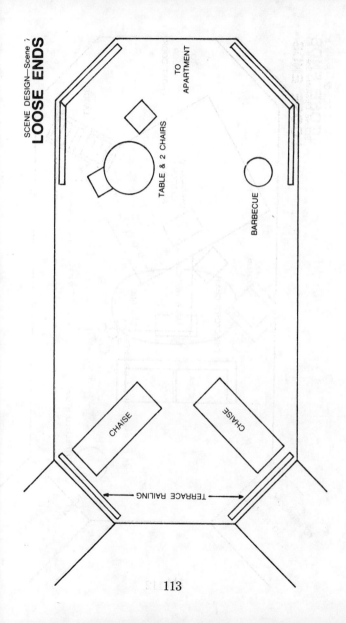

SCENE DESIGN—Scene 7
LOOSE ENDS

TO
APARTMENT

TABLE & 2 CHAIRS

BARBECUE

CHAISE

CHAISE

←— TERRACE RAILING —→

113

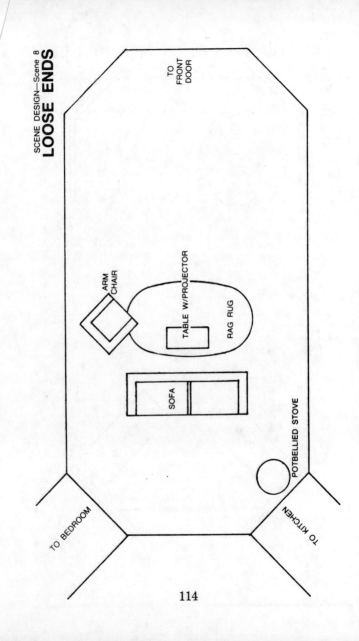

SCENE DESIGN—Scene 8
LOOSE ENDS

TO FRONT DOOR

ARM CHAIR

TABLE W/PROJECTOR

RAG RUG

SOFA

POTBELLIED STOVE

TO BEDROOM

TO KITCHEN

Other Publications for Your Interest

MAGIC TIME
(LITTLE THEATRE—COMEDY)
By JAMES SHERMAN

5 men, 3 women—Interior

Off Broadway audiences and the critics enjoyed and praised this engaging backstage comedy about a troupe of professional actors (non-Equity) preparing to give their last performance of the summer in *Hamlet*. Very cleverly the backstage relationships mirror the onstage ones. For instance, Larry Mandell (Laertes) very much resents the performance of David Singer (Hamlet), as he feels *he* should have had the role. Also, he is secretly in love with Laurie Black (Ophelia)—who is living with David. David, meanwhile, is holding a mirror up to nature, but not to himself—and Laurie is trying to get him to be honest with her about his feelings. There's also a Horatio who has a thriving career in TV commercials; a Polonius who gave up acting to have a family and teach high school, but who has decidedly second thoughts, and a Gertrude and Claudius who are married in *real* life. This engaging play is an absolute *must* for all non-Equity groups, such as colleges, community theatres, and non-Equity pros or semi-pros. "There is an artful innocence in 'Magic Time' . . . It is also delightful."—N.Y. Times. ". . . captivating little backstage comedy . . . it is entirely winning . . . boasts one of the most entertaining band of Shakespearean players I've run across."—N.Y. Daily News. (#15028)

(Royalty, $50–$40.)

BADGERS
(LITTLE THEATRE—COMEDY)
By DONALD WOLLNER

6 men, 2 women—Interior, w/insert

"'Badgers! . . . opened the season at the Manhattan Punchline while Simon and Garfunkel were offering a concert in Central Park. In tandem, the two events were a kind of déjà vu for the 60's, when all things seemed possible, even revolution. As we watch 'Badgers' we can hear a subliminal 'Sounds of Silence'."—N.Y. Times. The time is 1967. The place is the University of Wisconsin during the Dow Chemical sit-in/riots. This cross-section of college campus life in that turbulent decade focuses on the effect of the events on the characters: "Wollner's amiable remembrance adds up to a sort of campus roll-call—here are radicalized kids from Eastern high schools, 'WASP' accountancy majors who didn't make Harvard or Penn. Most significant is the playwright's contention that none were touched lightly by those times . . . he has a strong sense of the canvas he's drawing on."—Soho Weekly News. If you loved *Moonchildren,* you're certain to love this "wry and gentle look at a toubled time" (Bergen Record). (#3998)

(Royalty, $50–$40.)

1542   2191